The Otherworld

by James Hingley

Copyright

Table of Contents

Prelude

The Black Forest, 1297

'Siehen Sie etwas, Arbogast? Arbogast?'

'Beruhigen Sie sich.'

An unnatural quietness seemed to have gripped the forest, nary a whisper from the wind above them, nary a cry from the baleful crow which had dogged their steps ever since their entrance into this dark domain.

The two men of God had journeyed into this arboreal realm with a single purpose, and should they be martyred in their cause, then His will be done.

Their venture had taken them through field and meadow, hill and dale, until finally they had come to the hamlet itself. There, they had laid eyes upon her. A girl of four-and-ten years, her flaxen hair lying limp on the pallet bed that had served as her final resting place, her bloodied neck wrapped as best as the woodsmen had been able to manage, yet all to no avail. Addressing them through a veil of tears and torment, the maiden's mother had described her daughter's last moments on God's earth. She had spoken of a demon of the forest, one which, doubtless through the devil's magic, had sought to take on the appearance of a woman.

The devil had been forestalled in his evil, however, for his efforts had failed to fully achieve their purpose, God having rendered her skin a tunic of cobalt ash.

The folk of the hamlet had clasped the men to their breasts, thanking them for their bravery, and kneeling in prayer that, through their victory, He might deliver them from evil.

By dusk, they had reached the forest, their stout hearts momentarily chastened by the doleful wall of beech and alder that seemed to serve as a final warning against entry. They did not heed it. Into this dark world did they tread, armed with crucifix and sword, faith and dagger, the folk heroes of their youth strong in their memories. They sought a grove wherein, it was said, this affront to their Lord God had thought fit to make its lair.

Onwards, ever onwards, into the heart of the forest. Everywhere did bark and leaf appear twisted and sickly, as though what evil now trod this land appeared to have infected the very nature around it. The young monk began to silently affirm his faith in his Lord and the Blessed Virgin, for he felt the frailty of human weakness beginning to plague his wary soul. Ahead of him, his mentor strode forward manfully, fearing no devil or beast to come.

'Ich höre etwas...' said the novice. Indeed, he did hear something, a whispering through the trees. The wind? He was not sure. 'Haben Sie das gehört?'

His brother monk's rigid posture, inclining his head to listen, informed him that he too had heard the otherworldly murmurings ahead of them.

The older man turned, gesturing with his head to follow. Cautiously, they edged their way nearer to the siren's call, step by step, until their hands cleared a path through a dense thicket of leaves.

Before them, they saw a grove of light within an otherwise fortress of darkness, a stream trickling from some underpass hidden from view. They were startled, heads rising sharply, as a flutter of wings fled from the canopy into the world of light somewhere above. The elder monk's shoulders sank in relief. 'Ein Vogel'.

Upon finishing his utterance, the air itself seemed to come alive with what now sounded like a hiss, loud and incessant, flooding their ears unrelentingly. It was almost intolerable, their hands clasped tightly against the side of their heads in a desperate effort to protect themselves... then it ceased.

'Hubert', asked the man softly, 'Was war das? Hubert?'

He turned, frowning at the sight of his young companion fleeing into the trees from which they had entered. After a moment, he jolted, coughing a sudden flurry of blood. He felt something being pulled from his chest, then he fell heavily to his knees, his body being enveloped from both sides by demonic wings. As he stared ahead of him, dazed by his death blow, his eyes slowly moved to meet whatever fiend had delivered the strike. As he took in the ashen figure before him, he prayed to God to end his life now, so that he might be spared the horror to come.

1
Washington State, 2023

The tap water ran down James Carlson's face in cold droplets, disappearing amidst the soft fabric of the towel as he dried his now smooth skin. He stared into the mirror, the reflection of his tired eyes locked in a battle with his own. 'Come on, just one more day; you can do one more day, you've got to.'

Every morning seemed harder than the last, a leaden weight anchoring his soul in some bleak place deep within. He couldn't see a way back out. Most days, he found himself wondering why he kept going, kept bothering to shave, put on his uniform, and step out the front door. He didn't have an answer. Maybe there was none, he considered; a being of organic tissue being led on by chemical forces over which he had no control. Did he like what he did? At one point, he would have said yes. He wanted to help people, as trite as that sounded. Now, hell, he just wanted to see the next sunrise, to accept what was, what would forever be, and to stop letting his grief affect his performance on the job.

He picked up a photo of a woman, his sullen gaze taking in her smiling, happy radiance. He placed it back down, then readied himself for work. You can't keep doing this, he told himself, you've got to get back on the path, let the past lay buried.

After stepping outside and twisting the key, he heard muffled voices from two doors down, a cracked window bringing news that Sophie's new boyfriend was back. He watched as the door opened, a muscle-bound low-life revealing himself as his neighbour's latest burden. She appeared in the doorway, her pale hand held softly against her right eye, glancing with her panicked left, daring to tear her terrified gaze from the bully who deigned to call her his own. The man's head turned, meeting the stare of the six foot one, blue-eyed Army veteran of twenty-five. 'Fuck you lookin' at?' he spat.

'Did he hit you, Sophie?' he asked calmly.

Her eyes shifted nervously to the man beside her. 'It's okay, James, it's—'

'Bitch, shut the fuck up!' hissed the man.

'Hey!' said James, raising his voice and closing the distance between them. 'Did you hit her?'

'What if I did, you piece of shit?' came the reply, his upper lip curling in amusement, the foul stench of alcohol and weed causing James to grimace in disgust.

'Not man enough to answer?'

The man's nostril's flared, showing crusted mucus amongst a forest of hair. 'Yeah, I did, just like I'm going to do to you, bitch!' His right fist shot forwards, stopping dead as James caught him by the wrist, twisting his arm until he doubled over, whining as they always do, begging him to ease off. He slammed him against the railing, curious passersby stopping in the parking lot to watch the commotion. 'Put your hands behind your back!'

'Fuck you!'

'Just do as he says, Rick!' urged Sophie.

His hands struggled with the flailing skin, finally managing to get the handcuffs on him, glad to be able to step back from the odour of cheap deodorant and God knew what else. 'Alright,' he said, taking a few breaths. 'As of right now, I'm arresting you for battery and assaulting a police officer.'

'Oh bullshit!'

'Want me to call the paramedics to look at that eye, Sophie?'

The young woman shook her head sadly. 'I'll see to it, James, and... thanks for your help.'

The man glared menacingly at her as James led him past, then down the steps to the parking lot.

Six hours later, the door of the patrol car slammed shut as the impressive bulk of his partner, Steve Harris, settled down in the front passenger's seat. It had turned into one of those days. First, time spent processing Sophie's abusive ex-boyfriend, then later a call out for another of Bill Hayton's drunk episodes – the usual bout of yelling, threats, apologies – and now half an hour spent in assisting with the arrest of a three-hundred pound perp who didn't know the meaning of giving up.

'I gotta start lifting more,' remarked James.

'I've been telling you that for years,' replied Harris.

'I'm not talking Mr Universe heavy, Steve, just enough so that an incident like *that* doesn't happen again. The thing was a farce, him rolling around like that, his girlfriend shrieking her head off, and what was with the taser? Did it break?'

'Nope, it worked fine, it's just that some folks can shrug the electricity off, must be genetic or something; it's nothing you did. If you don't mind me saying so, James, you've been edgy all day.'

He stared out of the window, letting out a deep sigh. 'You know, it's two years to the day that she died.'

'Shit... I didn't know that. I'm sorry, man, I shouldn't have said anything.'

He waved a hand dismissively. 'There's no reason you should've remembered; she wasn't your wife.'

Harris glanced at his partner, realised that his words would be better left unsaid, and began to check his phone. 'Whole world's becoming crazier and crazier by the day. Says here that this country is fixing to go to war against another... I didn't even know the latter existed.'

'Genetic, you said? About the taser?'

He nodded. 'Yep, that's what I read.'

James considered this for a few moments. 'The older I get, the less I think I know about anything.'

'Look at you talking about becoming older. You're still in your twenties, James; come talk to me in six years.'

He smiled slightly, forgetting about past torments.

'Now, I'm only saying this because I need to let her know, I wouldn't do so otherwise, not on this day of all days. Thing is, my offer for Saturday night is still on the table. Emily says her friend is all ears about you, is eager for a double date, just saying.'

'I appreciate it.'

'But you're not gonna come?'

'I need to think about it, Steve. I know that Katie would want me to move on, but... it's easier said than done.'

He put up a hand. 'I get it, say no more.'

'So,' he said after a few moments, making the effort to smile for his partner's sake, 'What does she look like?'

Steve smiled. 'That's the spirit, I'll text you her number.'

'I appreciate you trying to help me, man, honestly, I mean it. Between us, I've been living in, how can I put it, a kind of mental prison since I lost her. I mean, I'm functioning, I'm here doing my job.'

'Right.'

'But it's like my mind's numb. I'm on autopilot travelling through a grey world, if that makes sense, as though its been drained of colour.'

'I can't pretend to know what you're going through, James, but, for what it's worth, it sounds like a normal thing to go through after losing Katie. The colour would go out of anyone's life.'

'Yeah, but I don't know if, in my case, it's coming back any time soon.'

'Don't give up hope, partner,' he said, slapping his hand on his shoulder cheerfully. 'Just see what this weekend brings, okay?'

'Okay,' he nodded firmly.

Their conversation was interrupted by a woman's voice crackling on the dispatch radio, then becoming more audible. They listened as the call went out: passing hikers had claimed to have seen a panicked woman desperately slamming her hands against a window from the second storey of a residence. The address was an out-of-the-way country house thirty miles east of Seattle.

Given their description of the woman as early twenties and red haired, it seemed possible that this was Amanda Collins, a college student who had gone missing two weeks prior on the way to her mom's house.

James's heart rate began its steady rise as the patrol car raced to its destination. This was not his first rodeo. He had been a deputy for three years now and had experienced his share of domestic violence call outs, disorderly conduct, even a bank robbery. This would be one more bout of adrenaline on an already experienced body, though a respectful caution was always in the back of his mind.

Once on the scene, they found that they were the first responders on site. Backup was on its way, but for now it was up to James and his partner to save the life of the victim.

'Here we go,' grunted Harris, 'shotgun out the back, body-cams on.'

'On it,' said James as he hurried to the trunk and made ready the black Remington 870.

The noon-day sun shone on the large, two-storey wood-built house, by all appearances derelict for years. Harris fixed his gaze on the windows, but the drawn curtains on every window bar one showed no movement. A suspected kidnapping didn't require a warrant for entry – no time for legalities – and speed was paramount. Harris's powerful form, having earned him the affectionate nickname in the department of their 'golden-haired buffalo', followed as James took the lead on approach.

His controlled, deliberate movements contributed to his status as the model deputy in his county.

Scorched yellow grass from the summer heatwave lay ragged over the cracked path before the sheltered front porch. The two deputies took up position on either side of the front door, thankful to be shielded from the attention of a relentless sun, courtesy of an unseasonably hot September.

'All right, try it,' instructed Harris.

Slowly, James tried the door, found it unlocked, and with a nod from Harris they made entry into the front hall. 'Sheriff's department!' rang out from the two young men.

Silence.

None of the sounds that they had anticipated hearing. No shuffling from a startled perpetrator in the adjacent rooms; no frantic cry for help from a kidnapped college student.

'Sheriff's department! Come out to the sound of my voice!' called James.

Not a sound.

They began to search the house, room by room. A potent mix of tension, excitement, and stress that most folk could never understand filled the body of James with each new door through which he passed. Each room a new possibility for a flag-draped funeral. Be it insurgents half the world away, or American citizens of his own state, James was here because he could manage these feelings, could show grit and keep himself steady.

He was good at what he did, but it would never be routine, and it would forever be a world that demanded respect from those who entered it.

Not a soul did they find in the dark, flashlight-swept rooms that at one point in time would have been a realtor's dream, but now resembled so many crack dens infesting the land. Littered newspapers, glass, a few needles on the carpet in front of the hearth. Nothing for it but to press on upstairs.

They knew that the silence around them meant that either the suspect was absent, hiding, or waiting in ambush behind one of the four doors on either side of the landing.

'Sheriff's department! Tell us where you are!' cried Harris, it not having gone unnoticed that they were yet to make contact with the suspected victim described over the radio.

Three empty rooms searched, one room left all the more threatening for it. If a kidnapper was waiting for them, then this would be where. Two firearms facing the door, its cross-shaped pattern seeming so incongruous in this foul, ill-boding place. Harris tried the door, swung it back into the room, and both men crossed the threshold weapons raised.

'Ah shit,' winced Harris. They had been prepared for a revolver-wielding kidnapper making his desperate last stand, but not the sight with which their faces now strained to maintain eye-contact. It was some sort of altar, if such a horror could be called by that name. On each side of a long, mahogany table, lay chained a young woman, naked and red of hair.

She was bound under her arms, her hands having been severed and placed either side of the table's surface. The macabre sight struck both of them dumb. Dried blood painted her lifeless body from chest to ankles. Red blood thrice formed the meaningless words on the wall behind which she lay: '*Math'ok Kalah Ak'esh*'.

James shook his head, then turned once more to the woman. 'Mam?' He felt like an idiot for saying it, yet he felt compelled to see if she had a chance, as obvious as the bleak answer was.

'James, call it in,' said Harris as he sought to compose himself, 'What is this?'

'Some sick shit, Steve; she's gone. Dispatch,' James pressed his radio, 'No suspect present, female DOA.'

'All right, let's see to...' said Harris, 'Shit!'

James only managed a half-turn before he felt the impact of what seemed like a bull knock him against the altar, his back aching from the impact, blood quickly trickling down his scalp. The cause of the impact, paradoxically as it seemed to him, was a tall emaciated man, bald with wild-eyes. His gaze was that of a rabid animal, darting from side to side as the being to which it belonged took in the figures of the two deputies before it. James saw Harris level his sidearm at the assailant, shouting at him to put his arms above his head, but the latter simply sneered in what struck him as amusement.

He had seen criminals run, posture, fall to their knees crying, but never had he witnessed a shout from a Glock-wielding cop arouse mirth in the man staring down the wrong end of it. The man crossed the three-and-a-half yards to Harris in a mad dash. Before he could react, blood was pooling from his carotid artery, the intruder's mouth clasped against his neck one moment, rising again before sinking downwards with tremendous force, blood staining his pale chin.

'Shoot him!' came a horrified scream from Harris, his body visibly becoming weaker by the second, his bloody hands seemingly unable to resist the attacker's grip in spite of his uncommon strength.

James saw his shotgun on the floor in front of him, reached for it, turned on the cold wooden floor, and saw the mad eyes lock with his own. What transpired took less than a second. James raised his weapon, saw the seemingly feeble body of the assailant drop Harris to the floor, lurch towards him, and he felt the vice-like grip of the man's hands around his throat. James's mouth contorted in tense anticipation of the same treatment meted out to Harris, almost unable to comprehend his situation out of shock at what was happening. He gripped the cold, corpse-like hands around him, unable to free himself from their grasp. Why had he not been bitten yet? What was this psychopath waiting for? He glanced with desperate eyes at his assailant, finding that he was being studied with the same look of calm curiosity that he had seen before.

'Soon,' rasped the man in an accent unknown, his breath stinking of flesh and blood, '*Al'esh th'kür.*' She was the key to our path. Yours is ours. Your kind shall witness what is to come,' he smiled, 'But not you".

James watched in horror as this babbling freak's teeth grew before his eyes, sharp grey needles being lowered to his throat. This thing was savouring the moment. Savouring it for too long, for in its anticipation of the kill to come, it had failed to heed James's hand movements, his Glock pointing directly into its chest. James emptied the cartridge, pulling the trigger like a madman. He fell back suddenly onto the floor, gasping for breath, and relief flooded within when he saw the hole-riddled figure collapse before him, blood oozing from its blown-off jaw.

2

James stood by one of several patrol cars on the road. Behind him, newly arrived men and women of the department were busy making their way to and from the crime scene. He had been in shock, so they told him, when backup had finally arrived, but now he was beginning to try to come to terms with what had happened.

Harris was dead, he hadn't needed them to tell him that, and he had been killed in a manner that he simply found hard to comprehend. Bitten to death? How had the piece of shit managed to get close enough to do that? How had he got to them without being heard? What was he on?

These questions dogged his mind incessantly as he waited for Sheriff MacAskill to make his way over to him. He could feel grief swelling inside his heart for his partner, his friend, but he knew from past experience that the way that suited him best was to suffocate it as much as he could.

"How are you holding up?' asked MacAskill, a dark-eyed, mustachioed figure, popular in his county and among his people.

'I'm holding, sir.'

'Well I'm glad you got the SOB. Hell, I'da shot him myself even if you hadn't," he spat, 'Scum like that don't deserve prison.'

'No sir.'

'I'll tell Steve's family, don't feel like you need to see to that, there's no shame in it, and sometimes it's better that way. I speak from experience.'

He eyed the ground, unsure of how to respond. The truth was that he was glad to have the responsibility of informing Carol, Steve's wife, taken from him. He looked into his sheriff's eyes, 'Sir, what happened in there wasn't right.'

'It never is, you know that.'

'No, sir, I mean...it wasn't *right*. The way that piece of shit moved, it wasn't normal. Harris should have been able to stop him, his pistol was pointing right at him, but somehow the bastard was on him before he could register it. He got hold of me the same way; I barely got a shot off before he did me in.'

'The heat of action can affect your sense of time, Harris's sense of time, it can happen. I liked Steve, James, as much as anyone, and so you know that it's no slur of mine to say that even he could make a mistake.'

'No, sir, he did everything right, but this was something else.'

Their conversation was interrupted by the arrival of a grey sedan about twenty yards away. James watched as MacAskill walked over to the car and shook hands with the man who stepped out. The latter looked like he belonged on Wall Street, light-brown hair immaculately styled, suit likely costing more than James's car, but he noticed that this would-be stock-broker was carrying a sidearm in a holster. A badge was flashed, MacAskill raised his hands in protest, more words were spoken, a cell-phone was offered to MacAskill, then James's eyebrows raised as he saw a rare display of acquiescence from his boss.

Two black SUVs arrived, accompanied by an equally gloomy-coloured transit van, more men stepped out, their clothing being markedly different: black BDUs without any identifiable markings. James had no idea who these folks were, but apparently they carried enough authority to walk onto MacAskill's crime scene unimpeded.

'Can you believe this?", asked the sheriff as he stomped back to James, "Twenty-seven years and I've never experienced a farce like this.'

'What's happening? Who are they?' asked James.

'Claim to be federal agents, National Defense Agency, whatever the hell that is. Say they'll take over, can you believe that? I tell them that it's my jurisdiction, so James Bond over there pulls out his phone, says a higher authority would disagree with me, and lo and behold it's Governor Chase on the line instructing me to do as they ask.'

The two men watched as the new arrivals made their way onto the property, carrying what were clearly body-bags, as well as large grey hold-alls filled with who knew what.

James bristled, 'You're really going to let them take the reins on this, just like that?'

'Wait until you're up for reelection, then you can talk,' MacAskill growled.

After ten minutes, during which time the sheriff had overseen the exodus of his deputies from the building, James watched as three sagging body-bags were carried down the porch and then loaded into the van.

'The hell do they think they're doing?' exclaimed James, furrowing his brow as he started towards the parked vehicles.

The man in the suit turned at the sound of running feet and raised his hands placatingly. 'I know what you're going to say, deputy, and rest assured that your partner will be driven to the coroner as is required.'

'Then put him in the back of an ambulance as normal, you son of a bitch.'

'James,' barked MacAskill, placing his hand on his shoulder.

'That's all right, Sheriff,' replied the man, now meeting James's stare with an equally intense gaze. 'Deputy, there are reasons for the transportation taking this form, no disrespect is intended towards your partner from me or my men, quite the opposite in fact, and I once again give you my word that he'll be driven to the coroner's as normal.'

22

'You're going to allow this, Sheriff?' James glared at his boss.

MacAskill hesitated, then narrowed his eyes. 'If I find out that Deputy Harris's body isn't present at the coroner's by this evening, you're going to regret it, understood?'

'Understood,' replied the man with a firm nod, and with that he turned to leave, the strange convoy departing, James feeling sick to his stomach.

***

That evening, he found himself sitting in his apartment, the lights off, trying to stop his mind from racing into a black pit of despair. It seemed impossible. Today was the anniversary of Katie's death, and while he had never been the best of husbands, he loved her, he always would, and he doubted that it would ever get any easier. Now, with Steve's death, it was all that he could do to keep himself from going to find a bar. He had promised himself that he wouldn't, he had made the same vow to Katie before the disease ate away at her, but now... screw it.

He put on his jacket, locked the door, and within minutes was on the road, cruising for a place to drown out the images in his head. He pulled up outside The Blue Lighthouse, his usual haunt. Andrew, the owner, poured him a beer, then he sat himself down at the bar to wallow like old times.

'Rough day?' asked Andrew.

'The roughest'.

He nodded, turning away to give him privacy.

After about twenty minutes, James decided that the shadowy figure in the corner of the bar was indeed watching him. He had shrugged it off as paranoia at first; it wouldn't be the first time that an old suspect had recognised him in his off-duty attire. But no, this wasn't paranoia; the woman hadn't stopped staring since he had sat down. Finally, he turned to look, challenging her to maintain her gaze. 'Something wrong?'

She shook her head, taking a sip of her drink, a slight grimace appearing as she swallowed.

He turned back around, reasoning that perhaps he had been mistaken, though knowing full well that he hadn't.

A few more beers, then the realisation that he had driven there. Damn it. Did he have enough for a taxi? He peered into his wallet. Shit. He sighed irritably. There was nothing for it, he would have to walk back.

It was dark now, the long summer nights just a dream until the coming year. He passed a few couples who smiled, enjoying their happiness together, and he cussed himself out for having had the stupid idea to go out tonight at all. God! He had been doing so well; his sobriety was well and truly out the window.

After he had been walking for about fifteen minutes, he heard footsteps behind him, staggering as he turned around to look. It was the woman from the bar. She stopped, staring, her black hair flowing from under a red hoodie, her face half-shrouded in shadows.

'Can I help you?' he asked.

He saw her lips form a smile, then her head tilted to the side, gesturing towards an alleyway to her left.

He looked, saw the alley, and turned back to look at her. 'I'm married... was married. You'll have to find someone else tonight.'

He turned to walk on, yet only managed a few steps before he was once again thrown through the air, landing about ten yards to his left, penned in by both walls of the alley. He was dazed, bruised, panting for breath. The alcohol had been bad enough for his vision, but now his whole world seemed to be spinning; a sick merry-go-round of a nightmare.

He managed to steady himself, grabbing his bleeding head with both hands. God it hurt. His collar was then grasped by the woman, lifting him upwards as though he were a child. This couldn't be happening, not again, not in the same day.

She tilted back her hood, revealing the same wild eyes that had taken Harris's life that day, the same look of pure malice and ill intent. He grasped her wrists, applying all the strength he had, but still she would not let up. He felt her choking him, his vision becoming blurrier and blurrier. He heard her spit a series of words at him, but he couldn't make sense of them, and soon he felt darkness beginning to overtake him.

He was desperate, he needed air, now. He felt himself falling, his body slamming against the ground, the world becoming black around him. Before the light was shut out, however, he noticed the woman fall also, figures on the side-walk rushing over towards them, and a man's voice telling him that he would be okay.

3

In spite of the grey drizzle that had accompanied him this last half hour, the smartly dressed man had a good feeling as he casually ascended the steps to the third floor of the apartment complex. His records had informed him last night that this was the address of the lucky deputy who had done what few novices – and in his line of work even a SEAL was a novice until initiated – had managed to do. He was no stranger to recruiting personnel for the NDA. He knew how to charm, how to appeal to the ego, but the truth was that most agreed precisely because they realised the price at stake if they didn't.

James slowly eased himself off the couch as he heard the doorbell ring for a second time. What time was it? He checked his watch: 11:45am. What the hell happened? How had his forehead become bandaged? He remembered the bar, the strange woman, even the struggle in the alleyway, but everything else was blank. Somehow, he had ended up back in his apartment that night, but as to how, he was at a loss. The doorbell rang again, just as he was reaching for the lock. He opened it and was taken aback by who he saw.

'Deputy Carlson?' the man grinned, 'Agent Calvin Ford, National Defense Agency, we met at the Faircastle residence. Sorry for dropping by unannounced, but I was hoping to discuss an opportunity for career advancement if you're available.'

'How did you know my address?'

'Sheriff MacAskill was good enough to oblige me.'

Ford had never blanched at lying if it was for a good cause, and he knew that soon Carlson wouldn't mind anyway.

'I see,' muttered James, eyeing this suave walking grin in front of him, 'and you said you were from which agency again?'

'The National Defense Agency, and before you say it, I know, you've never heard of us, not many have, and the government aims to keep it that way.'

If not for his appearance at the house of horrors, and MacAskill's acceptance of him, then James would have told Ford exactly where he could go. As it stood, he invited him in.

'Nice, I like your décor,' remarked Ford as his eyes took in the baseball memorabilia adorning the walls, the half-patched leather sofa, and what he took to be the previous night's dinner on a tray nearby.

James sat down heavily on the couch, reclining his arm over the back. 'Yeah, well, I don't usually like to stay in much, more of an on-the-go kind of guy.'

Ford gently set his suitcase against the wall to his left, 'You and me both, but I take it from your use of 'usually' that things have been different since we last crossed paths?'

'What do you think?' James's eyes narrowed disdainfully, 'I watched my friend get his neck torn apart by a psychopath, that tends to leave a mark on you.'

'I don't doubt it,' stated Ford thoughtfully, his attention still being directed more towards the apartment than to James, 'And a man with fangs to rival a python's isn't something you soon forget.'

James looked up at Ford, finding the man's eyes now staring fixedly at him, his cheerful expression having been replaced with one of serious intensity. 'MacAskill told you that too, huh?'

'No,' replied Ford, 'Not at all. You see, Deputy Carlson, the suspect whom you dealt with was not a stranger to my agency.'

He eyed Ford with curiosity. 'You mean you know who he was?'

'We know *what* he was,' Ford pushed out his lips in thought, 'As for his name, it was probably unpronounceable anyway.'

'*What* he was?' asked James, 'You mean a gang affiliation?'

Ford smiled. 'Of a sort. As you found out last night, this gang has other members.'

He frowned. 'What do you know about last night?'

'I know that you went out to a bar, got drunk, and almost got yourself killed again. I also know that me and my team saved your life and brought you back here, so how about a thank you?'

'What are you talking about? Saved my life?'

He nodded. 'I'd say so. I mean, I've had rough dates before, deputy, but it looked like love wasn't the thing on her mind.'

James stared at him, his eyes hard. 'Look, I have just had the worst day-and-a-half of my life. My partner's dead, I almost died yesterday, twice if what you say is true, and so if you know more than you're letting on, then out with it.'

Ford stopped smiling, momentarily adjusting his posture. 'Listen, there's no way to tell you this without risking incredulity on your part, and that's okay, that's normal, all I ask is that you hear me out until the end, and that you know beforehand that what I'm about to tell you is the honest to God's truth, I swear it.'

James straightened before gesturing for Ford to continue.

'You've probably never heard of a place called Highgate Cemetery,' he began, 'It's a graveyard over in London. Back in the late sixties, it became something of a sensation for the folks over there, talk of black magic, the discovery of a headless woman's corpse, and their very own Van Helsing delving into a crypt to strike at what lay within. Flash forward twenty years to Catalonia. Spanish newspapers are in a frenzy at numerous disappearances of six young students, four of whom were never found, two of whom ended up as bloodied corpses in a low-end apartment.' He paused to glance around

30

him. 'Reminds me of something actually.' He smiled upon noticing James's irritation. 'These are just two examples of cases involving the particular kind of assailants you found yourself facing recently, and I hate to say it, deputy, but stranger tales have been told. The Beast of Bray Road, the Hopkinsville Goblins—'

'The Chupacabra,' interjected James, not without a hint of derision.

'No, actually that really was just a case of coyotes with mange. No, what I'm saying to you is that there *are* monsters out there, Deputy Carlson, those you have faced throughout your career, those like the ones you faced yesterday, and those that you have yet to meet. If I say vampire then you'll say bullshit, you know it and I know it, but you also know what you saw, what that thing did to Harris and almost did to you. You saw how it moved, you know that it wasn't human, you just need to take the next step and accept the obvious.'

'Vampires,' James muttered, 'I see. All right, Agent, what was it? Ford? I've heard enough. You want to fuck about after what I've been through, be my guest, but you can do it some other place.'

'You can call it whatever you like, what matters is that it existed, and more like it exist, them and a whole host of freaks that ten years ago both of us would have laughed away.' His demeanor shifted back to his casual self, 'At any rate, why do you need me to convince you? Technology can finish my job for me.'

He calmly unpacked a laptop from his suitcase, plugged in a USB stick, navigated to a media player, and turned the screen for James's benefit.

James watched as body-cam footage played in front of him. The camera was attached to one of ten men, all wearing the black BDUs and balaclavas that he had seen worn by those at the crime scene. The location appeared to be a hotel hallway, the men, all heavily armed with automatic weapons, making ready to enter one of the guest rooms. James watched wide-eyed as the men kicked in the door, entered the room, and immediately began to fire upon the individuals inside. James felt a knee-jerk reaction to protest, no call for compliance having been heard, no weapons being visible on those being gunned down, but then he saw their teeth. Hell, he could see them for the fangs that they were, two or three inch needles visibly declining in size as the men and women lay sprawled on the floor. He couldn't deny that what he was seeing, whatever these people were, whatever they were on, they resembled snarling nightmares made flesh. The footage ended soon after the corpses had been zipped up in body bags and carried out of the room.

'We dealt with the cell at Highgate in the same way, and the high-born 'lord' in Catalonia. Rest assured, they would do infinitely worse to us if they had their chance, you've seen that for yourself. The Ak'esh – vampires to you and me – are one of the greatest threats to our planet, you can trust me on that, and if you want a hand in stopping them, stopping them from doing what they did to Harris, then you'll have a place with us if you're interested.'

'*Ak'esh?*' James said, "I heard that word when the bastard had me, he uttered some gibberish about a gate, and Amanda Collins being the key.'

'I read your report,' stated Ford with interest, 'We don't often get to chat with his kind, it's usually a shoot-first-then-burn kind of deal, and I'm not the only one whose curiosity has been aroused by its words.'

Ford paced the room for a few moments, then returned to James. 'There's nothing for you to sign, firstly because I don't think there's any need when it comes to you, and secondly because no one would believe you anyway. What you do next is up to you. You can go back to being a sheriff's deputy, patrol your county, maybe hope that you'll somehow forget what you now know, hope that you don't run in to what you know is out there. That woman last night? She was an Ak'esh, sent to take revenge against you for killing ol'skinny McGee back at the house. Something to think about. Alternatively, you can call me on this number,' handing him a card, 'And join the only fight that matters.'

Later that day, after dusk had settled over the parking lot outside, James sat in his apartment eyeing his phone and the sheet of paper bearing Ford's contact number. He typed in the digits, then deleted them. He shook his head ruefully with a grin, 'God, this is nuts.' His mind was an endless stream of considerations, dismissals, and counter-questions. Was he really contemplating phoning this guy? Fella spun a good tale, no doubt, but vampires? Monsters? This must be a joke, he thought, it must be.

Yet there it remained in the back of his mind, that ever present word 'what if' pulling him back to the topic at hand. What had happened had happened, he couldn't deny that, couldn't shake his head and pretend he hadn't seen the inexplicable with his own eyes. What answer did he have other than Ford's? Nothing that stuck, nothing that eased his doubt.

Time passed; he found himself looking at Katie's photograph. What would she have said to all this? He knew that she wouldn't have been dismissive, not at first, not with the curious mind she had always had. He smiled at the memory of her that came to him, her hand clasping his, laughing as she pulled him closer to the ledge, then the two of them jumping on 'two', a sea of warm water engulfing the image. What future did he have here? It *was* real, he knew that. He knew that he had a choice to make, one way or the other.

He hesitated for one more moment, picked up the phone, and dialed.

'Ford,' the voice on the other end answered.

'I'm in.'

'I know.'

4

Four days later, James was sitting in his car outside Seattle-Tacoma International Airport. The fluttering leaves landing on his wind-shield seemed like a good omen to him; a time of change for nature, a time of change for him. He hoped that this was the right call. It was just time off, for now; MacAskill had understood that given the circumstances.

Barely an hour had passed these last forty-eight hours without the question 'What are you doing?' entering James's head. His reply had invariably been that if what Ford had said was true, and this really was the world that he was living in, had always been living in, then he would rather take a proactive part in his own defense. He was scared, more so than he remembered ever having felt before. It was that fear that had driven him to this parking lot, waiting for the appointed time for his rendezvous with Ford. All that he had been told was to bring the bare minimum, the rest would be provided for.

His watch showed 9:30am; like clockwork, he heard a knock on his left-side window. It was Ford, accompanied by an auburn-haired, bespectacled young woman dressed in jeans and a bomber-jacket. James got out of the car, locked it, and shook the waiting hand.

'Allow me to introduce Agent Järvinen, one of our intelligence analysts,' said Ford cheerfully, gesturing towards his companion.

James met the handshake proffered by the woman. 'Good to meet you, Agent...Yar-venen?'

'Järvinen,' she corrected him politely in an accent that suggested Minnesotan, 'My old man's Finnish, and it's good to meet you too, Deputy Carlson.'

'You can call me James.'

'James then. My name's Anna.'

Ford eyed the two of them with satisfaction, not unlike a parent taking pride in having planned a successful play-date. 'Well, now that we are all acquainted, I think we have a flight to catch.'

The twin-engine jet had not come as too much of a surprise to James. A government agency could hardly expect to court new talent by flying coach. As for what else transpired during that almost five hour flight, nothing could prepare him for it.

'Alright, let's get started,' declared Anna as she organised a series of folders on the table in front of her. She was sitting directly opposite James, with Ford reclining on the other side of the aisle, listening intently as always. 'Agent Ford has informed you of the true nature of the beings that attacked you, the truth behind some of our long-held-to-be myths, and has invited you to join the NDA as a field operative.'

James nodded. 'Correct.'

'Good, my job is now to get you up to speed. I suppose it makes sense to start with what you've already seen.' She consulted the leftmost folder, drew a laminated photo from it, and turned it to face James. The image before him showed a freeze frame of more body-cam footage, seemingly at the moment when the would-be attacker was in the act of lunging towards the cameraman. The same jaws, bloodshot eyes, and pointed ears as before, except this thing had evidently been hitting the gym prior to this.

'What you see before you is an Ak'esh,' explained Anna, 'Or more commonly known as a vampire, although we now know that they are merely one of a number of sects or bands. Much of what you know from folklore bears truth; they do indeed subsist off human blood, or blood in general, and they are subject to extreme burning in sunlight, even to the point of death, although a cloudy day does allow them a reprieve of movement. We don't know how many exist on Earth at any one time, though we estimate that it could be in the hundreds; it fluctuates.'

'Fluctuates?'

'Yes.'

'Where do they come from?'

'A place that is officially known as the 'Trans-dimensional Access Zone', yet unofficially we call it the Otherworld.' She smiled sympathetically. 'If you need a moment to get your head around all this, that's all right.'

'Yeah, that's... a lot to take in.'

'I felt the same way; it can take a bit to absorb everything.'

'How long have we known about all this?'

'That's still an open question. We know that people throughout the world were aware of the existence of otherworldly beings since at least the time of the Roman Empire, almost certainly before. We have tracts, chronicles, and treatises over the last two thousand years that describe all manner of things we used to think were legends. That was until the year 1908.'

'1908?'

She nodded. 'Yes, that's the year that the forerunner to the National Defense Agency was founded. You see, Edward Cartwright was a Secret Service agent who happened to encounter one of the Ak'esh while on vacation in northern Maine. Like you, he was able to kill it, and he was then able to inform the government of what he had encountered. Theodore Roosevelt was hesitant to believe Cartwright's story, of course, but fortunately Vice President Fairbanks revealed his own encounter with what he termed a 'wolf-man' in his youth. Roosevelt saw that they were sincere, agreeing to set up an agency to investigate the claims. Over time, with a lot of mistakes made along the way, that agency gave birth to the National Defense Agency. From outward appearances, the NDA exists as just another organisation tasked with pursuing criminal investigations on behalf of the federal government. Our real mission statement, however, is to monitor, track, and pacify all threats that come through to our world.'

'And that's what you were doing with Harris's body? Protecting our world?'

'We returned his body as promised,' said Ford, 'But he had been bitten by an Ak'esh, so we couldn't take any chances. Not all the things you've read are true, but humans *can* become one of those things. It's rare though, they prefer killing us outright.'

'Do other countries know about all this?'

'Most do, to varying degrees,' Anna replied, 'And various sister-agencies exist throughout the globe, though none are larger than the NDA.' She smiled proudly. 'We are the foremost protective wing this planet has against a threat most don't even know exists.'

'You were talking about this Trans-dimensional...?'

'Trans-dimensional Access Zone, or the Otherworld, yes. It's where the Ak'esh, werewolves, Shrouded Ones—'

'Shrouded Ones?'

'Picture a human with blueish to grey skin, iris and pupils a void of black, sharpened teeth, a taste for human flesh...'

'I must've missed them in folklore 101.'

'They're rare, but bad news if you're unlucky enough to meet one. As I was saying, they enter our dimension through portals, for want of a better term, originating from what we term the Otherworld.'

He lowered his head, eyes-widening. 'You're kidding me?'

'Really? Portals are the thing you find hard to believe?'

He sat back, folding his arms. 'No, sure, portals, please continue...'

'They appear at random, adhering to no discernible schedule that we know of, but always somewhere secluded, usually deep in a forest or rarely trod mountain range. Once they're here, in come their inhabitants, though never more than one or two at most.'

'How do you know all this?'

'Well, once we learned where they tended to appear, we could plan for their arrival. We have hundreds of observation outposts scattered throughout North America alone, with teams whose sole task is to monitor and report their appearances if and when they occur. By following this tactic, we've been able to intercept several incursions before they made headway into our world.'

He raised his index fingers to interject. 'Right, so, where exactly is it that they're coming from? I know you call it the Otherworld, but what is it? Another dimension, you said?'

'We believe so, yes, but why the portals appear and disappear, we don't know.'

'Has anyone ever gone through to this Otherworld? I mean, if they can come to our dimension, presumably we can go to theirs.'

'The portals don't remain open for more than a minute. From what I understand, the higher-ups have considered sending an expedition through, with the aim of learning more, perhaps stopping the portals altogether, but they never commit to it.'

'Why not?'

She arched her eyebrows. 'Would you want to go to where vampires call home?'

'Right, stupid question.'

'So,' chimed in Ford, 'Our job is containment: monitor incursions into our world, track the spread, and pacify it. If possible, learn anything to our species' advantage.'

'Oh?' James asked, 'Such as?'

'Well, for starters, trying to understand the physiology of these beings, what makes them what they are. Take the vampires in general. We don't know how long they can live if left to their own devices, but we have pacified individuals that appeared to be linked to cases several hundred years in the past. Imagine if you could study such a being, learn how it managed to live for so long, the possibilities would be endless.

'But that's all still academic, since, as you know Ford, we've yet to crack that mystery.'

'Hey, a man can dream.'

'So,' James said, raising his hand, 'You've explained how they get here, but you haven't told me what they're purpose is in coming.'

'That's because we don't know,' replied Anna. 'We know that they tend to be highly dangerous towards humans, often feeding from us in some shape or form, and we know that for some, such as the Ak'esh, they have an organisational structure. You have to understand, in all the decades that our organisation has been in existence, we've never managed to capture a living specimen.'

'Never?'

'Never,' she replied, 'Not one that lived for very long afterwards anyway.'

'The woman from the bar, she seemed to understand me when I spoke to her.'

'Oh they learn our languages well, they seem to have some kind of mental advantage when it comes to that. In so far as they learn it, however, it seems to always be out of a desire to lure in their prey more easily.'

'And that's what I was going to be? Her prey?'

'We suspect that she was aligned in some way with the Ak'esh you killed at the Fairbanks residence,' replied Ford. 'How she tracked you down beats me, but then they're crafty bastards; just look at how your kill got the drop on you.'

'I still don't know how we didn't hear him...'

'Evidently you didn't check the floorboards.'

'The floorboards?'

'Oh yeah, floorboards, chimneys, I've seen one that had a hollowed out compartment inside a mattress; they'll think of all sorts of places that you never would.'

Ford excused himself for a moment, returning a few minutes later to announce that they would be arriving shortly.

'Where are we headed?' asked James.

'Monroe County Airport, Indiana,' he replied. 'Then its about a half hour's drive to NDA headquarters in Morgan-Monroe State Forest.'

5

James stared out of the window of the SUV, seemingly watching the traffic pass by as they made their way along the I-69, busy trucks driving to their drop-off points, the mundane nature of their task seeming comical in light of all that he had learned.

He still didn't know if he believed all that he had been told. In the back of his mind, he was still half-expecting the cameras to pop out of a nearby bush, a microphone thrust towards his face, some minor celebrity informing him that it was all for a reality TV show. If so, he thought, it would be one hell of a show, since the other half of his mind was convinced that this was legitimate. It was hard to tell whether Ford was every being truly serious, but Anna seemed genuine. When he factored in the footage he had seen, as well as Ford overruling the sheriff at his own crime scene, then the hairs on his back rose at the realisation that this was all too real.

'One thing that's bugging me,' he said to Anna, 'It's the twenty-first century; how is the internet not crawling with photos of these things?'

'A few reasons. Firstly, the internet is a lot more regulated than you think, James, not officially, of course, but unofficially the government has methods of removing the more glaring images that pop up online. Secondly, if a regular person ends up encountering a being from the Otherworld, they rarely live to tell the tale, so it's rare that any feel comfortable enough to get out their phone and start filming.'

'Good point.'

'Thirdly, and it really is this simple, people are incredulous in this day and age. They're more likely to call 'fake' on a genuine image of an Ak'esh or Shrouded One than they are to believe it.'

They turned off the interstate, leaving the stream of cars and trucks behind, the country roads becoming more rural by the second, their path marked by farm houses, oak and ash trees standing a silent watch over the landscape. Soon, he saw the expanse of thick canopy ahead, marking out the beginning of the state forest. Once more, they changed roads and drove along a forest path, then another, the latter narrower, more overgrown, not the sort of place a hiker would want to tread. The path slowly curved to the right, whereupon they were immediately faced with three armed guards, their uniforms a dark grey, a leashed German Shepard rising eagerly on its hind legs upon seeing them.

Ford rolled down the front passenger's window, holding out his identification for inspection. 'Special Agent Calvin Ford, accompanying Special Agent Anna Järvinen and Deputy James Carlson.'

The guard nodded. 'We were briefed concerning your arrival, Agent Ford, go straight on through.'

'Thanks,' he replied, pocketing his ID before casually signalling to the driver to move on.'

After continuing on the path for another five minutes, passing through a second checkpoint along the way, the vehicle turned onto an open expanse of tarmac within the forest, the area fenced off, a large concrete building standing a lonely vigil among bark and ferns.

'Welcome to Sandalwood; home sweet home,' remarked Ford cheerfully.

'Welcome to Sandalwood, James,' said Anna.

The driver waited behind as the three visitors walked to a guard post adjacent to the front entrance, once more explaining their presence, then entering the building. Within, James was surprised at what he found. He wasn't sure quite what he had been expecting. Perhaps the guarded checkpoints and grey uniforms had given him an anticipation of entering Dr Evil's lair, but what he saw looked more like the main floor of the New York Times. Ordinary men and women, most in smart office attire, were milling around, as though on a coffee break.

Ford sidled up to a reception desk, asking the woman behind it if 'the chief' was around, to which she replied that she would inform him of their arrival. They waited for five minutes, James taking in the whitewashed walls, medium sized offices adjacent to the lobby, and finding himself noticing Anna staring at him. She saw that she had been noticed, smiling and turning away bashfully, then footsteps announced the arrival of a higher-up.

'Prompt as always, Ford,' remarked a tall, thin man with thinning grey hair, hazel eyes, and an accent that reminded James of a Boston Brahman.

Ford cocked his head to the side rakishly, 'We can't all be Mr Perfect, sir, but I come close.'

'And modest too,' he smiled thinly, then holding his hand out towards James. 'You must be Deputy Carlson? Director Edward Van Houten, it's good to meet you.'

James shook the man's hand, thanking him for his invitation.

'Well, really, the pleasure is mine, deputy. I have had a look at your record: four years in the military, a distinguished combat record, an able law enforcement officer thereafter, and now one of a small group of alumni who can boast to have ended the life of an Ak'esh. Frankly speaking, you're just the sort of man the NDA is interested in meeting.' He cleared his throat before continuing. 'If we could speak briefly in my office?'

'Of course,' James replied, Ford and Anna remaining behind while he followed the director into a lift, down to a lower floor, and along a hallway into a large office full of awards, commendations, and family photographs.

'Please take a seat,' gestured Van Houten, taking a deep breath. 'I'll be frank with you, Deputy Carlson, you appear to be a marked man.'

'You're referring to the woman... the Ak'esh that attacked me on the street, sir?'

He nodded. 'There is little doubt that she had deliberately targeted you in revenge for your having killed another of their kind. I cannot in all honesty say that you are safe, Deputy Carlson.'

'Call me James,' he interjected.

'I cannot say that you are safe, James. It is possible, yes, that her death might be the end of the matter, yet our experience is that vampires as a rule are a proud, remorseless species, very determined in their efforts to seek retribution over the course of years, decades even, if need be.

'You're saying that I'm still danger?'

'We are all in danger every moment that we share an existence with their kind. You, however, as is the case for all who have crossed paths with the Otherworld, are particularly at risk. I do not mean to frighten you, but you will likely forever be a target for them, forever a wrong to be righted.'

James nodded slowly. 'It really was one of those days...'

'Hmm?'

'Nothing, sir. So, where does this leave me?'

'You have three choices. You may leave, return to your life as a deputy, and take your chances. You may enter into a special form of witness protection: a new state, new identity, daily monitoring by the NDA for your own safety.'

'And the third is to become a field operative?'

'Precisely. You have the requisite training, both military and law enforcement. You appear to possess the right temperament, nerve, and, what is more, you have shown yourself able to successfully fight back against those who would do you harm.'

'I got lucky the first time; the second time I ended up being half-choked to death.

'You had been drinking heavily, I am told?'

James shifted uneasily. 'That's true.'

'There would be no shame had you been stone cold somber.' He leaned forward. 'Listen, we will train you to confront the Ak'esh, as well as an all manner of insurgents from their dimension. You will not be alone, you will be part of teams of other specialists, all trained as you will be. You will be tasked with mopping up an ever spreading wound, so to speak, but we have been doing this for many decades now; you will not regret your decision.

James momentarily looked down at the desk, then raised his head to firmly meet Van Houten's eyes. 'Well, looks like I'm in.'

The director smiled. 'I'm glad to hear it. Now, let's rejoin the others and explain more about what we do here.'

James followed as the director, accompanied by Ford and Anna, took them deeper into the facility. It was clear that it was an exceedingly deep structure, with at least eight levels as far as the elevator could be trusted, but James somehow had a feeling that there was more left unseen.

Soon, they came to a large chamber, with rows upon rows of staff seated at computers, all leading up to two cinema-screen sized monitors at the very end. Upon the latter, James stared at more footage of SWAT-style raids against monstrous beings that he couldn't identify. In another, a helicopter kept pace with some sort of hairy creature that roared upon feeling the sting of a dart fired from above.

'This is our surveillance room,' explained the director. 'It's where we monitor the body-cams of our operatives, as well as keeping in contact with our networks of observation stations for signs of activity from the Otherworld. In addition to this,' he smiled, 'We have have access to a nationwide surveillance network, connecting to all public closed-circuit cameras in North America, hence how we were so recently able to monitor your movements and prevent your untimely demise.'

'That was very good of you. Tell me, is all this legal?'

'It's not something that I would concern yourself about. We are sanctioned by the highest authority this nation has, and by and large most of our actions fall within the framework of United States law.'

'Well, it's certainly extensive, I'll give you that.'

'It needs to be. Most of the creatures and beings we deal with are wary of humans. They bide their time when it comes to their interactions with us, aware that our numbers make us a force to be reckoned with.'

'Do you ever lose people?'

'Unfortunately, yes, we do. I am afraid that it is as inevitable as suffering casualties in a conventional war. Please, follow me.'

They progressed through further halls, the director nodding to various colleagues whom they passed. 'This next room is our barracks for teams stationed in the central United States, allow me to introduce you to some of those whose ranks you are joining.'

They stepped into a large room, similar in appearance to the barracks that James had lived in during his army days. Two men stopped chatting and walked over to the director, eyeing the visitors with interest.

'James, allow me to introduce you to Special Agents Crawford and Murphy.'

James shook their hands, the former being a tall, well-built man in his mid-thirties, his hair greying at the temples, his eyes sharp, calculating.

'We heard about you from the rumor mill, James,' said Murphy with a friendly smile, his green eyes and firm handshake exuding warmth. 'I'm sorry about your partner, but we couldn't help but be impressed that you took out an Ak'esh all on your own.'

'I got lucky.'

'Hell, there's luck involved every time we go up against the bloodsuckers, that don't change a thing; I'm glad to shake your hand.'

'Crawford and Murphy are some of our most experienced field operatives, James. I am assigning you to their group, of which Crawford is in command.'

'Glad to have you aboard,' said Crawford.

James nodded, 'Glad to be here. What kind of equipment do we have access to?'

'M4s, thermoplastic ECH, ballistic vests. You'd be better off asking what we don't have access to.'

'No silver bullets?'

He smiled thinly. 'Regular bullets do the job just fine.'

'There are also these,' said Murphy, 'lifting a square, yet far from rigid piece of material from his pocket. 'It's a neck guard, protects us from getting some of the more brutal hickies you can imagine.'

'Any of these combatants in the habit of shooting back?' James asked.

'Some, vampires mostly. Even they seem to have a tendency to want to close in though, use their natural weapons rather than ours.'

'We believe that, aside from the obvious desire to feed, foregoing firearms might be a facet of their culture which we don't yet understand,' said Anna.

'Culture?' Crawford scoffed. 'They're just animals in need of putting down, nothing more.'

'Well, sir, with respect—'

'Regardless,' interjected Van Houten, 'James is probably in need of some down time on account of his journey and recent experiences. He can learn more about the facility later. For the meantime, may I formally extend our welcome, Special Agent Carlson.

6

A month and a half later, James made ready his carbine as the helicopter flew low above a mass of dark, Appalachian woodland.

It had been fifty-five days of lessons in combat tactics, target identification, and survival training that had all aided his efforts to adapt to the strange new world in which he found himself.

Now, he felt a flood of relief that he was finally taking part in an operation. The call had gone out at half past four that night. Police in Huntington, West Virginia, had received reports of a bloodied camper stumbling around the city limits. She had been in shock, repeating herself over and over, stating that her boyfriend had been attacked by something akin to a monstrous wolf or bear, but insisting that it was neither. Crawford and his team had been assigned to fly to the area, using thermal imaging to see if they could locate the assailant.

'You ready for this, Carlson?' asked Murphy with a thumbs up.

'Ready as I'll ever be.'

'Just remember, it ain't rocket science, you see a giant bipedal wolf, you blow it to hell, got it? It'll be on you in seconds if you give it a chance, and at that point we can't help you.'

'Got it, thanks.'

Murphy grinned. 'Any time, brother.'

'Got something!' came a shout from the co-pilot. 'Thermals are showing a large signature moving through the undergrowth, far bigger than any bear I've ever seen.'

'All right,' said Crawford, holding his hand to his ear as he spoke through the headset. 'Bravo Team, have your pilot set you down a mile south of the target, work your way north from there. Charlie you take the west, Delta you're east. Pilot?'

'Yes, sir?'

'Set us down a mile north of here, we'll work our way south and head it off.'

'Copy that.'

The chopper gained speed as it flew north, descending rapidly and hovering above the ground in an open area of felled oak and pine, the downwash blasting twigs and leaves in all directions. Once on the ground, the eight men of Alpha Team took up positions along a thirty yard stretch, with three or four yards between them, covering the tree-line south. Their ears soon adapted to the quiet around them, broken only by the distant humming of the chopper's blades.

'Pilot?', Crawford said, the helicopter having disappeared from sight.

'Sir?'

'Do you still have a visual on the target?'

A few moments passed, then the familiar voice confirmed that the mass of yellow heat signature was still making its way rapidly in their direction, charging through logs and branches as though they were nothing.

Crawford signalled to his men to ready themselves. James looked through his sight at the woods beyond, not a movement to be seen among the wall of timber and pine needles standing silently before him. A few heads turned to see what Crawford was thinking. He sensed that their eyes were on him. 'Easy, hold your positions.'

Gradually, James perceived a noise in the distance, one of crashing branches echoing through the forest. It was growing louder by the second, clearly coming their way. He gripped his weapon more tightly, focussing his aim, aware of the need to remain calm and control his breathing.

Still nothing.

'See anything?' came a voice in his ear.

'Can't see shit,' replied another, clearly on edge.

'Should be on you in twenty seconds,' came the co-pilot's voice.

'Where the fuck is it?' someone asked.

'Stay calm, boys, hold it together...' said Crawford. A brief pause. 'Contact! Open fire!'

Nothing could have prepared James for the sheer speed of the monster that burst forth from the forest, leaping a distance of twenty yards as though it were nothing, teeth ripping into Nichols, their medic. In moments, there was nothing left but the dying echoes of a deluge of lead, all to no avail, for the beast had carried Nichols off into the forest, his desperate screams becoming ever distant by the second.

'Fuck!' yelled Crawford, now breaking a silence that had only been punctuated by the heaving of chests as adrenaline surged through their bodies.

'Command?' spoke Crawford into his earpiece, 'I have one man MIA; target is on the move,' then letting his arm drop, 'God, what a mess. You all right, Carlson?'

James remained stunned by the intensity of what had happened, turning to look at his commander, taking a moment to register what had been asked. 'Yes, sir... I'm all right.'

'Then let's move, all of you!'

Without another word, the squad reloaded and were moving swiftly through the trees behind the clearing, entering a world of louring pine, ferns brushing against their legs, all minds focussed on saving Nichols from a grisly fate. James felt the shock leaving him.

His heart was still pounding, his breathing heavy, but his desire to save his squad member seemed to override any thoughts that he might have had for his own safety. This was what he wanted, he felt; this was why he had joined the NDA.

'Do we have a visual on the target?' Crawford shouted into his headpiece.

A burst of static, then the pilot's voice informed him that it had stopped about a hundred yards ahead of them. Guided by their eyes in the sky, their muddied boots made their way around trunks, both fallen and standing, the darkness of the world below the canopy, as well as their ever closer proximity to the target's last location, slowing their movement little by little.

Their sprint had led them to a mine entrance formed of shattered, age-worn planks of wood, now dangling from the impact of the combined mass of monster and man having crashed through its half-rotten barrier.

'Shit,' said Murphy, 'Fucking shit...'

'Command,' reported Crawford, 'Target has entered an abandoned mine, request permission to pursue?' The next few moments seemed to last a lifetime. 'Copy. All right, NODs on, controlled movements, don't let this thing get the drop on you. Murphy, take point.'

Without hesitation, Murphy stepped forward, his night-vision display illuminating a light-green dirt track beyond the entrance, debris littering the ground, flecks of already drying blood mixing with the dust of a former century's labour.

Merely a minute passed before they came to a fork in the tunnel's path, Murphy pausing to wait for Crawford's decision. It was decided that Crawford, James, Schweitzer, and Johnson would take the right fork, Murphy, Rogers, and Henriksen the left. Without further orders, both teams set off on their separate paths, both sharing the same anxious thought that somewhere, behind the next turning, death awaited them.

James had been made pointman for his fork. He could scarcely remember when he had last felt this alert, this focussed. He wondered how far into this black pit Nichols had been taken, whether he was still alive… whether there was any hope for him even if he was. After passing through a long stretch of tunnel, making every effort not to cough from the swarm of dust particles that seemed to infest the air like a plague, James raised his right hand high. The others stopped. They, too, had heard the sound. It was faint, akin to a whimper. It was something, and so onwards they pressed, their pace as fast as they dared move.

The whimper died away, replaced by a sudden, heart-stopping snarl that resounded throughout this cavernous hell into which they had delved. It was nearby, they realised, and James hastened towards the source of the sound, his ears straining, turning left and right to follow the new path calling him forward. Another left turn, a chamber long ago carved out of the earth, and before their eyes, a great mass of fur and muscle rising and falling with every sinister breath. It didn't seem to notice their presence. Slowly, taking each step as silently as they could, the four men began to surround the creature.

It only took a few steps for James to see the grim sight of Nichols. The beast was eating its way through his ravaged throat, a look of shock and dread etched on his ghostly-white face, his once clean uniform stained a bright crimson, his neck a gaping chasm where once had been fine skin and muscle. He grimaced, a terrible anger building up inside him, fueling a desire to give vent to a newfound bloodlust, as wild and primordial as that which flowed within the soul of the beast itself. As though of one mind, the four men opened fire, riddling the beast's back with bloody entry wounds, its bulk rising upwards in shock, the men taking a step back, then relief overcoming them upon the sight of it collapsing heavily on top of the dead man.

As James's sense of hearing returned, he began a cautious approach towards the now motionless being. He had seen images of werewolves back at headquarters, but they paled in comparison to the horror of the real thing. It struck him as more pig-like than canid, its long snout more akin to that of a boar than a wolf, but its fur and claws spoke the truth of its identity all too well. He couldn't believe it.

There was no time to dwell, however, with Crawford letting off another burst into the animal's side for good measure. Together, with the rest of the squad that had run to their aid, they pulled the beast, all one-thousand two-hundred pounds of it, off Nichols.

'God...' Murphy uttered, his face grim.

'Poor bastard,' said another.

James looked away, puzzled at a curious mix of emotions within him. He grieved for the loss of his squad mate, of course, yet there was more, much more, to how he felt in this moment. Perhaps it was the adrenaline, he thought, but, and he felt ashamed to say it, there was an unmistakable sense of elation within him. He felt good. Was it the triumph of the victorious warrior? Maybe. All he knew was that, for the first time in a long time, he felt as though he could see the world in colour once more, that the greyness had lifted, that he had perhaps found the purpose that he was looking for.

'At least you can see, Carlson, why we do what we do, no matter the risks,' said Crawford.

A murmur of agreement went out from the other members of the team.

Outside, the other squads had linked up with them, with members of Charlie busy setting a controlled fire alight, Delta and Bravo having been tasked with hauling the freak of nature out of the mine, then overseeing the destruction of its body.

'We've got enough W's on ice not to bother with this one,' explained Murphy to James, the two watching on as the creature's fur began to burn, its skin and muscles starting to sizzle, blacken, and emit a pungent smell to rival a garbage dump. One thing was still on James's mind, however, and he thought now as good a time to ask as any. 'Say we'd been able to save Nichols, would he have turned into one of those things?'

Murphy shook his head. 'It doesn't work like that, James.' He gestured with a nod towards the smoking remains of the werewolf. 'There's no human in that thing, there never was. What comes through from the Otherworld is what you see, an animal, a sick parody of what a wolf should be, nothing more. Had we saved Nichols, he might have recovered, but my advice? Don't think about it. I'm surprised he wasn't killed outright when it landed on him, that thing weighs more than a grizzly bear.'

They carried Nichols' body to the landing zone, loaded it onto one of the awaiting helicopters, and one by one they took off on the journey back to Sandalwood.

7

The following afternoon, James waited in the lobby of Sandalwood, checking his watch to make sure that he hadn't forgotten the time. 12:36p.m. It was on her, not him, he thought with a smile.

He looked up as a door swung open, a keen-eyed Anna appearing from behind it, flushed, as though she had been running. 'Sorry!' she said as she came up to him, 'I didn't forget, I just got caught up with some data that came in.'

'Don't worry about it,' he smiled, 'You said we'll take your car?'

'Yeah, I know all the shortcuts once we're out of the woods and onto the highway. Do you like coffee?'

'Sure.'

'I know a great diner: Mama Joe's, it's in town, not far, so if you fancy getting back soon it's not a problem.'

'Anna, I'm just happy to be getting out somewhere, it's fine.'

'Okay,' she said, nodding, 'Just thought I'd give you the option, you know?'

She drove them to the outskirts of Martinsville, the sunlight on their cheeks a welcome change from so many hours spent underground.

After pulling into a largely empty parking lot, adjacent to an even emptier business park, they got out to find a seat at the diner. James glanced at the building's red brick facade, its sign depicting a cartoon of a plump woman pouring steaming black coffee, thinking how quaint it was to be back in the world he knew so well. They didn't find many patrons inside, only a tired parody of the artist's rendition of the owner, and two truck drivers reminiscing about old times, but James was glad for the privacy.

'So, I've been meaning to ask,' he said after they had sat down in the corner of the room, Anna adjusting the salt and pepper in front of her, 'How did you end up in the NDA?'

'Oh,' she smiled, 'It's the typical story; dad wanted a boy, encouraged me to join the military like he did, so off I went, straight into the Army after college. Ended up in intelligence; guess my scores were good, and I was never the best at PT.'

James smiled, enjoying her company. The owner's footsteps announced her presence; both turned and met her steely gaze. 'Ready to order?'

'I'll have a coffee with scrambled eggs and bacon, please' said James.

'I'll have the same,' replied Anna.

The woman took their menus and beat a hasty retreat.

'So,' she continued, 'I completed my required years of service, then got recruited into the CIA.'

'How'd that see you switch to the NDA?'

She shrugged. 'I guess someone higher up must have liked my work, since it wasn't as if I applied, no one does, we're all recruited into it.' She chuckled. 'Maybe someone read my internet history and saw how many 'mysteries of the unexplained' type websites I liked to look at.'

'Oh?' he grinned.

'Yeah, I know it seems amusing now, given all that we know, but at the time I couldn't get enough of that stuff, always waiting for the next blurry photograph of the Loch Ness Monster or Bigfoot to turn up. It's cringeworthy, I know.'

He put up a hand in protest. 'Nah, it's... well it's kind of cute actually.'

She smiled, eyeing the table. 'And you?' she asked, looking up, 'What's your background, James?'

He took a breath. 'Well, I come from a small county a few miles west of Seattle. Mom ran out on us when I was nine, never saw her again.'

Her expression became more serious.

'After that, I spent years waiting until I could get the hell away from my dad, or at least until I was big enough for him not to take a swing at me anymore.'

'Jesus...'

'It's all right, I don't hold too much of a grudge anymore, I've moved on from all that.' He sighed. 'Anyway, we both share a past in the Army. I was in the 75th Ranger Regiment, did my time in Afghanistan, then left in '20; I seem to have a habit of not staying too long in one place.'

'Then you became a deputy after leaving?'

He nodded. 'Yep, figured I was suited for it, able to keep my cool in intense situations, or I like to think so anyway.'

'You never married? Had a girlfriend?'

He looked to the side before answering. 'I was... but she died.'

Anna frowned in surprise. 'Oh, James, I'm so sorry, I didn't know.'

'It's all right. She had cancer; it was the two year anniversary of her death back in September, on the very day I entered into all...this.'

'I'm sorry.'

'I appreciate it. It's nothing that I ever thought I'd have to go through, and I've been through hardship in my life, but nothing like that; I wouldn't wish it on my worst enemy.'

'What was her name?'

'Katie,' he smiled.

'You must have loved her very much.'

'I did; I still do.'

She nodded.

'I know that I have to move on though,' he said after a moment's silence. 'I can never forget her, never want to. It's just, allowing myself to stay in the past with her wasn't good for me. I realise now that it wasn't good for her either, not for my memory of her, I mean; it was becoming something painful when that was the last thing she would want it to be.'

She nodded sympathetically. 'I think I understand.'

He looked up, smiling. 'I'm glad. I like talking to you, Anna.'

She blushed. 'I like talking to you too, James.'

The moment was interrupted by the owner, her bright red lips pouting disapprovingly. 'Will there be anything else?'

'I'll have a refill on my coffee, thanks', replied James.

'Coming right up...' She returned, refilled his cup with an eye set firmly on Anna, then returned to her other patrons.

James smirked, 'Something I did wrong?'

'That's just how she is,' replied Anna light-heartedly, 'Adds to the atmosphere, I suppose.'

'So, what data did you say had kept you earlier?'

She glanced round to check that no one had sat near them. 'Well, it's pretty fascinating if I'm right. The Ak'esh that attacked you, Ford's report stated that it had written the words '*Math'ok Kalah Ak'esh*' in blood on the wall behind the victim.'

He nodded. 'I remember.'

'Well, it's not the only example we have of such words being left on the walls of Ak'esh hideouts. In the last two months, we've raided four different properties with Ak'esh writing on the walls, three of which had victims bound and ritually murdered in front of it.'

'Do you have any leads on what it means?'

'Not a clue. We've had linguists attempt to make some semblance of sense out of the Ak'esh language, but with nothing to go on, no vampire Rosetta Stone, we keep hitting a brick wall.'

'But clearly this '*Math'ok Kalah Ak'esh*' means something important to them.'

'Exactly! We just need to figure out what. There's more though.' She leaned in closer. 'We have multiple reports of a Shrouded One in the areas where these murders have taken place. Now, Shrouded Ones are rare at the best of times, I know of only a few instances in my entire career when we discovered a trace of one. Yet now we've had surveillance footage of one appearing in close proximity to three of the last four rituals.'

'You haven't been able to track it down?'

She shook her head. 'They're extremely secretive beings. You wouldn't think it, given their appearance, but they're able to hide their tracks and stay out of sight to an astonishing degree.'

'But you think it's connected to the Ak'esh killings?'

'It's far too much of a coincidence to ignore. Think of it this way, would you shrug your shoulders at a member of Al-Qaeda appearing at three out of four murder scenes committed by MS-13?'

'Point taken.'

'I urged Van Houten to make it our top priority for investigation, and I think he agrees, so fingers crossed.'

'It sounds like it's definitely worth looking into.'

'Thanks. So, I've been meaning to ask, how do you like it here?'

He looked around at the diner. 'Here?'

'No, I mean working for the agency. Was it what you hoped it would be?'

'It's looking that way,' he smiled. 'I think I wanted something to stop me looking inwardly all the time. I was doing a lot of that; it wasn't healthy.'

She nodded.

'And now that I've been part of it for a little while, been in the field, well I'm glad that I made the decision. What we do matters, I'd have to be a fool not to see that. I guess what I'm saying is that I have a higher cause to live for now, it's not all about me, and I'm glad of that.'

'I'm pleased for you, James.'

'Thanks.'

8

Two weeks later, James was once more in a convoy of operatives, this time in armored SUVs leaving a trail of dust in their wake. The full moon was masked by wisps of dark grey cloud, a Great Horned Owl twisting its head to watch with curious yellow eyes as the speeding motorcade passed along the secluded country road. The night air was cold, grasping the legs of Alpha and Bravo team as they stepped out at their destination.

Their destination was a homestead, roughly sixty miles west of Indianapolis, the agency's home turf. It had become a pattern for the NDA as of late. Intelligence would intercept a call to local law enforcement, in this case a request for a wellness check on the said property. Too many times now had such checks led to Ak'esh rituals being discovered, and Van Houten had authorised the recall of officers to allow his own operatives to investigate the residence.

James reflected on his conversation with Anna a fortnight before, not just thinking about how right he had been, how much he felt his state of mind improving as a result of his newfound purpose, but also about how he felt towards Anna. It was early days, he knew, and doubtless the NDA did not approve of employee relationships anymore than any other agency would, but still, he couldn't help but find himself smiling whenever he thought about her.

'Five minutes out,' said Crawford, his face severe. James noticed that he was glancing now and then at a photograph in his hand, one of a smiling girl in hospital robes, her head devoid of hair. He hadn't known that Crawford was a father, but then again, he considered, he had only really got to know Murphy well during his brief time in the NDA, never tiring of hearing the lighthearted New Yorker's jokes about his former escapades in the Marines.

The men prepared themselves, checking the readiness of their weapons, aware of the need to control their breathing.

Three minutes, two...

'All right, move,' snapped Crawford as soon as their vehicle came to a halt outside the property. The sixteen operatives of Alpha and Bravo team, weapons raised to cover the windows, proceeded to form a perimeter around the front of the homestead. It was a large, single storey building, blacked out inside, with a wide porch upon which swung a white rocking chair in the wind.

Their movements were practiced, Bravo continuing to cover the windows, while Alpha proceeded cautiously to the front door. They had no reason to suspect that anyone inside was alert to their presence. Silently, Crawford signalled to James to try the door. It was locked. James reached behind him to detach a black-headed sledgehammer strapped to his back. He prepared himself, watching as Crawford counted to three with his fingers, then he swung, the still quiet broken by the shattering of the front door, splinters flying either side of him, and the patter of footsteps as Crawford, Murphy, and the rest of Alpha made entry.

They swept the hallway and rooms immediately to their left and right. They found nothing but untouched rooms, nothing seemingly out of place, cushions on the furniture neatly made. They continued their sweep, electing to use flashlights lest their NODs restrict their line of sight. Nothing. The ground floor was empty, but that still left the basement.

Bravo remained outside to cover the property, lest a stray hostile try to make its escape. Once more, James tried the door, finding it unlocked. Crawford signaled for him to take point. After taking a breath, James slowly opened the door, the muzzle of rifle raised, and began to edge forward, down the dozen and a half of steps that led down into the basement.

His flashlight illuminated the steps before him, one by one, the wall covering his right side. He sharply turned left upon reaching the bottom, followed close behind by his team, Murphy's hand having remained on the back of his shoulder throughout the descent.

The intelligence had been right, it was another ritual site. Before them, they saw a bloodstained farm table, doubtless once brown, but now a crimson coat staining its tarnished wood. Upon it had been placed the severed heads of the entire family, unseeing eyes staring ahead, as if trying to comprehend the horror that had befallen them. Candles cast shadows that danced softly between the horror-stricken faces. The rest of their bodies were nowhere to be seen. In spite of the nightmare before them, one question remained foremost in the operatives' minds.

Where were the Ak'esh?

Crawford began to flank left towards the table, Murphy and the others moving right. James noticed, on the right of the room, the same literary spectre haunted them once more: *Math'ok Kalah Ak'esh* still slowly dripping from the wall.

'All right,' announced Crawford, 'Let's call it in—'

A tremendous crash of falling plaster and ceiling debris interrupted his words, a bald-headed nightmare, fangs dripping with blood, falling upon him from above. He was lucky, Murphy having had the confidence of aim to blast the vampire off him. Crawford hurriedly checked himself, patting his neck with his hands, nodding in thanks to Murphy. It proved to be premature, however, for more crashes resounded from the ceiling as half a dozen Ak'esh, wild-eyed, fangs gnashing like piranhas, some half-naked, landed on and around the operatives. One, a newcomer like James, was unlucky, two having fallen hard upon him, pinning him to the floor under their weight, ripping his neck guard away, blood spurting from his neck and staining the lampshade beside him. James turned to fire, but he was knocked to his right by a wiry assailant, its bloodshot sclera thrust against his own eyes, its breath reeking of death. He grappled with it, his ears ringing with the sound of gunfire resounding all throughout the room. His M4 had gone flying, so he resorted to the best weapon he had, his fist. Over and over he pummeled its face, trying not to make contact with its teeth, recoiling quickly when it would snap in its direction. It seemed to be working, he thought, feeling its grip weakening. With a final surge of energy, he pushed the Ak'esh backwards, reversing the tables so that it now lay on its back.

In one quick movement, his adversary still dazed from its beating, he grasped his weapon and delivered a bone-crushing blow to the vampire's face using the rifle butt.

He felt his chest heaving for air. He turned to assess the damage. A few more rifle shots entered the heads of already motionless Ak'esh, the surviving operatives making sure that there would be no more surprises for them.

'Status report?' Crawford yelled.

'Edwards is dead,' replied Murphy dejectedly.

'Fuck. All right, everyone sound off, I want to know if you were bitten and I want to know fast.'

The survivors all reported that they were unharmed, although a murmur went out that one had shit himself, gallows humor not being an uncommon feature of NDA field agents.

'I'll see to this myself,' said Crawford, striding over to Edwards, raising his rifle, and firing a single shot into the dead man's forehead. James understood; they couldn't take any chances. He turned as he heard a rasp from behind him, remembering that he had not delivered the coup de grâce to his erstwhile wrestling partner. He raised his rifle, then hesitated.

'What are you doing, Carlson? Get on with it,' snapped Crawford.

'Sir,' he said, 'We have an opportunity here.'

'What are you talking about?'

'We've been investigating these ritual sites for some time now, yet we don't seem any closer to making a breakthrough in understanding them.'

'There better be a point to all this.'

'Well, sir, here we have a chance at taking one of the Ak'esh prisoner; we can find out what he knows.'

Crawford bridled at the suggestion, but he hesitated in his response, seeing the others nod their heads and concur with James's logic.

'I think Van Houten would approve, sir,' said Murphy.

Crawford gritted his teeth. 'All right, zip-tie his hands, and for God's sake be careful.'

James was helped to secure the prisoner, a dark bag being placed over its head, its legs being tied up to prevent a struggle. He was carried to an awaiting SUV, then the convoy departed for Sandalwood after forensics had arrived to oversee the cleaning up operation.

The convoy's arrival at headquarters was greeted like the Second Coming. Van Houten could not shake their hands enough upon learning that Alpha Team had secured an Ak'esh prisoner.

'Well done, Crawford, well done!' he cried.

'The credit is Carlson's, sir, he subdued the prisoner.'

Turning to James in the lobby, Van Houten rushed to clasp his hand. 'I knew that we were right in recruiting you, James, there was no doubt in my mind that you were NDA material, and now you have proven it ten fold.'

'Just doing my job, sir,' he replied.

'You can be as modest as you like, James, but I can safely say that there will be a commendation in this for you, without a doubt.'

'Thank you, sir.'

Anna came running out of the building, keen to hear the news. Upon learning of their success, she had to restrain herself from hugging James there and then. 'You remembered what I said about needing a Rosetta Stone.'

'I did, so the credit is partially yours, Anna.'

She smiled. 'It was a team effort. Anyway, you had better go stow your equipment and change; you won't want to miss the interrogation.'

That evening, after having showered, changed, and been checked by a medical team, James stood in an annex of the communications centre, standing behind Van Houten, as well as a few other squad members, as communications officers sat in front of them and stared into a series of glowing monitors. The screens showed footage broadcasting from an interrogation room located on a lower level of the facility. Bright lights shone from above on the seated figure of the motionless Ak'esh, the bag still shrouding its face, four armed guards watching it from all four corners of the room.

Emerging shadows announced the entrance of Anna and Ford. They sat down at the table in front of the prisoner, Ford nodding to one of the guards to remove its head covering. The man stepped forward, grasping the top of the bag and pulling it off in one swift movement. The Ak'esh looked up, its sickly eyes darting about to comprehend its new surroundings, its torn rags and shoes markers of countless nights spent on the move, fleeing from daylight.

'Rise and shine, bud,' said Ford.

The dark pupils swept to meet Ford's eyes, pure hatred emanating from them.

'Do you understand us?' asked Anna, a notepad in front of her.

It met her gaze, inclining its head ever so slightly, almost politely.

'Good, that's good. Do you have a name?'

Again, it bowed in affirmation, this newfound dignity striking both agents as highly strange given their usual contact with such ordinarily feral beings.

'Are you willing to tell us what it is?'

Its lips widened slightly, revealing a thin smile between a flash of fangs. Slowly, it shook its head.

'All right,' said Ford. 'Let's get right down to it. You're our prisoner, understand? Where you are right now, there's no getting out, so you can put thoughts of escape out of your mind altogether. We know what you are, and we know what you need. Blood.'

The creature stared, listening, its eyes unblinking, a look of intense curiosity.

'You have a choice. You can cooperate, and we will provide you with the blood that you need to survive. You will remain a prisoner here, but you will live. If not, then you can stay fettered to that chair for as long as it takes for you to starve to death. We might even put a video on for you to watch, maybe footage of a slaughterhouse in operation; ought to make you feel real hungry.'

A look of irritation replaced its hitherto calm countenance.

'Well, what's it going to be?'.

Grudgingly, the Ak'esh raised its head to meet his interrogators once more. 'Ask...' came a dry, foul smelling voice.

'Why did you murder the owners of that homestead?' asked Anna.

'They are prey; as you do to yours, so we do to you.'

'There was more to their killings than a desire for sustenance. We know more about you than you think, and we know that arranging your victims' heads on a table, accompanied by candles, is not typical of your dining habits.'

It smiled a grin that sent shivers up Anna's spine.

'Tell us the meaning of *'Math'ok Kalah Ak'esh'*.

It's levity evaporated. It's upper lip rising in a snarl.

'Hey!' Ford yelled as he brought his hand down on the table. 'This isn't a negotiation, freak. You tell us what you know, or it's a slow death, that's the deal you've got. We know that there's a purpose to the writing, and that it's connected to these ritual killings you and your buddies are carrying out, so cut the silent act and talk. You're full on the blood of that family back there, but think about how you're going to feel in a day, a week, a month, however long you pieces of shit can go without feeding. Maybe then you'll decide that it would have been better to talk.'

The Ak'esh considered this, eyeing the table, clearly in thought. Slowly, it raised its head. *'Math'ok Kalah Ak'esh'* is our speech. In your tongue, you would say 'Let the Ak'esh be bringers of the flood.'

'Why write that on the walls at the scenes of your killings?' asked Anna, writing down the translation.

It tilted its head slightly, as though stating the obvious. 'The flood must come, and we must be its harbingers.'

Anna felt herself feeling a need to step outside for fresh air, the sheer stench of its breath making it hard to concentrate, yet she forbore to carry on. 'Is this flood connected with the Shrouded One?'

For a split second, something resembling fear appeared in its eyes. 'There is no Shrouded One.'

'Don't play dumb,' said Ford, 'We know she's connected to this. You've been here for long enough, you ought to have become aware of surveillance cameras by now.'

It grunted irritably. 'There is *no* Shrouded One.'

'Now you're lying.'

Without warning, the Ak'esh lunged forwards towards Ford, its chains breaking its momentum, its body snapping back sharply against the chair. Ford signalled to the guards to lower their weapons, all having been raised in alarm.

'Now I know that there's a Shrouded One involved, you wouldn't have reacted like that if there wasn't one. Might as well start talking, pal.'

'You are prey, as is your female. All of you,' twisting its head in anger, 'All of you are cattle, nothing more, and soon all your kind will know this truth.'

'How? We outnumber you, our technology is superior to your own, hell, you don't even have any, at least nothing that isn't originally ours.'

It started to laugh bitterly.

'What's so amusing?'

'Technology,' it cackled, 'Takes other forms.'

'It sounds as though you're suggesting that there's a plan to control the human population of Earth, is that what you're saying?' asked Anna.

'A plan? It is our destiny.'

'And the rituals are a requirement in accomplishing this?'

It turned its head away, its eyelids closing. It was clear that it would say no more.

'Maybe later you'll feel more like talking,' said Ford. 'In the meantime, I'll see if there's a rat around here you can eat.'

An hour later, James met with Anna, Ford, and Crawford, amongst other members of the NDA, to join Van Houten in the briefing room. They all felt tired to varying degrees, James especially, but warm coffee and the glare of ceiling lights helped to keep them alert as they took their seats around a long, oval table.

Van Houten entered, taking his seat at the head of the table, adjusting some papers before raising his head to address his staff. 'I applaud you all on a job well done; you have outdone yourselves. We now know, assuming that the Ak'esh was telling the truth, that the purpose of these ritual murders is to bring about some sort of subjugation of humanity. We don't know how, but we know that it is connecting with a 'flood'. What this means, your guess is as good as mine; it could all be nonsense, but I am of a mind to assume that there is truth behind it until we have additional information.'

'And the reports of the Shrouded One, sir?' asked Anna, 'The Ak'esh seemed to be fearful of the mention of it, which, as Ford said at the time, seems to suggest that there is substance to the idea of one being connected.'

'I am inclined to agree. At this point in time, I am instructing further examinations of all surveillance footage in areas surrounding the sites of Ak'esh ritual murders. If there's a Shrouded One in the vicinity, then we'll do our best to pick it up.'

'And the Ak'esh, sir?' asked Ford, 'What's going to happen to him?'

'We will keep him under observation, see if an ever decreasing source of blood will weaken his resolve, and then we shall see if he feels ready to provide more information on the identity of this Shrouded One, as well as his compatriots.'

'Nice work getting him to talk, Anna,' said James after the meeting had adjourned.

'Thanks, James. I don't mind admitting it, I was on edge in there. I know he was bound but, still, it's hard to sit there staring it face to face like that; your flight reflex is yelling at you to run.'

He nodded. 'Well, he isn't going anywhere any time soon, so we've got nothing to worry about.'

'True,' she smiled.

'Do you think you'll have much luck tracking down this Shrouded One?'

'Honestly, I'm doubtful of our chances. Like the director said, we'll do our best with what we have.'

'That's all that we can do.'

They parted ways, James heading to his quarters and falling into a much needed sleep.

He was awoken some time during the night, a wailing alarm sounding throughout the facility. He rose from his bed, flung his clothes on, pulled on his boots, and hurriedly opened his door. He was confronted by several armed guards rushing past him, right to left, with two members of staff fleeing in the opposite direction.

'What's going on?' he called.

'Containment breach!' came the reply, 'That thing's broken out!'

'Ah shit,' he muttered, rushing in the direction of the armoury. Upon reaching it, he found that others had had the same idea, with men rushing to and fro, those armed in his direction, those not in through the armoury's doors. Murphy was inside, handing out rifles and shotguns. 'James!', he called, 'Can you believe this shit? How the fuck did it breach containment?'

'No idea, it was bound tighter than Houdini.'

With this, James and the remaining men ran from the armoury, their footsteps forming an audible beat through the whitewashed halls and offices, along to the metal stairway, and down four flights of stairs to the interrogation room.

He almost tripped over a body as he rounded the corner from the stairwell, a blonde intelligence officer, he thought her name might have been Madison, lying dead with a chunk of her neck bitten clean off, her white shirt drenched in her own blood. Ahead of her, lay two more bodies, one of whom was a security officer who James recognised as one of the four guards from the interrogation. What the hell had happened?

They burst into the interrogation room, nine of them in total, and found the once plain, clinical walls now splattered with the blood and viscera of the remaining guards. It was a bloodbath, and there was no sign of the perpetrator anywhere.

'Where the fuck could it have gone?' asked Murphy.

'No idea, but we need to fan out,' said James, 'You four with me, the rest with Murphy; I'll take the left hallway, you check the other floor above us.'

'Copy!'

The two teams went their separate ways, James walking cautiously, but with a certain rapidity to his steps, the muzzle of his shotgun raised ahead of him at all times. He came to a doorway, then quickly lowered his aim as a frightened group of personnel fled from beyond its entrance-way. He kept up the pace, checking room after room, hallway after hallway, finding still more blood trails and lifeless corpses of familiar faces along the way. He couldn't believe that this had happened, and part of him began to feel deeply responsible. He swore for not having finished off that piece of filth when he had had the chance.

There was no point thinking about that now, he told himself; all that mattered was stopping its rampage.

He swept the entirety of his current floor, he and his team making their way back to the stairwell, linking back up with Murphy's team as they did so. The two groups now joined together to sweep the third floor, still more bodies turning up, some face down on the cold tiles, some leaning against the walls, their throats slashed, their necks bitten, one missing an eye. They must have been caught completely unawares, he realised.

After sweeping more floors, joined by additional field operatives from more distant parts of the facility, they came to a partially open door marked '*Surface Access*'. James entered first, finding a ladder that appeared to lead several floors up through darkness, a small, circular shaft of light illuminating his face.

'Oh my God...' said Murphy.

'Is this what I think it is?', asked James.

'Access to the surface, yes; it's for emergencies.'

'Well, looks like it found out about it somehow.'

'Christ...'

'Let's try to stop it becoming worse; follow me.'

Bar by bar, step by step, James climbed the sixty yards of ladder towards the small circle of sky above him, his firearm banging against his side all the way.

Once at the top, only fresh air and darkness greeted him. Not a trail, not a sign, nothing to suggest which way the escapee had gone.

Upon returning to the lobby, they were met by Van Houten and another squad. 'Well?' he asked urgently.

'It's likely he got out through the surface access tunnel, sir' replied James, 'But there's no sign of him after that.'

'God damn it! How could this have happened?'

'I suggest we check the security cameras, sir.'

'Right,' he said, collecting himself. 'Waterson,' pointing to a tall, dark-haired man to his left, 'Organise your men, have them search the surrounding woodlands, have helicopter support called in to provide thermal imaging from above. I want that creature brought back at all costs.'

'Yes, sir,' the man replied, gesturing for his team to follow him.

Murphy and James accompanied Van Houten to the surveillance room, finding that Anna, Crawford, and Ford were already a step ahead of them.

'It's no good,' Anna said, turning to meet them.

'What?' asked Van Houten.

'I said it's no good, sir. We've rewound the footage for the last two hours, but it turns to static for ten minutes before and after the incident.'

'How can that be?'

'We don't know.'

'Can it be fixed?'

'Doesn't look like it, sir,' replied Ford, his usual casual charm replaced by a commanding seriousness. 'Phelps is looking into it, but he's not hopeful.'

'How could it have got loose? It was shackled and bound to that chair with numerous padlocks, wrist, legs, even its neck. I was assured that it was as secure as could be.'

'It couldn't have broken its bonds sir,' said Ford, 'Nothing of our experience with the Ak'esh suggests that they're capable of that kind of strength. James there grappled with it and beat it senseless, so there's no way it was breaking through steel restraints.'

'Some other way then?' Van Houten suggested. 'A method of breaking the restraints that does not require strength?'

'Is it possible that someone freed it?' asked James.

Van Houten turned sharply. 'Freed it? I'm not in the mood for jokes, Carlson.'

'It's surely a possibility, sir, given how incomprehensible it's escape appears to be.'

'Who in their right mind would want to free it? They would have likely ended up dead on the floor of the interrogation room for their trouble.'

'I don't know, sir, but I think we'd be wise to keep it in mind as a possibility.'

'Duly noted.'

'If we can't find it, sir,' said Crawford, 'That means we have an Ak'esh that knows the location of this facility, which means others of its kind will also know.'

'I can't believe this is happening...'

'Sir,' said Crawford, 'Perhaps we should consider contingency plans.'

'You mean relocation?'

'Yes, sir.'

'You don't think that we can defend ourselves? We're a government facility, man.'

'It's not that, sir, it's just that, if we assume that the Ak'esh will be aware of our location from now on, they'll know to move their area of activity far from us, potentially target civilians in the area on the assumption that they might be NDA personnel.'

Van Houten sighed deeply, clenching his jaw. 'I'll make arrangements for it. God, I can't believe this has happened.'

After the other left to see to their duties, Anna approached James with a concerned expression. 'Are you okay?'

'Yeah, why?'

'I just wondered, that's all.'

'What do you rate our odds of tracking it down?'

'Honestly, not good. If it wants to, it could bury itself in the soil for days on end; we wouldn't have a hope of finding it. Now that it knows that it's on the run, I doubt that it'll be taking part in any more rituals for a while.'

'So we're screwed'.

'We'll keep up the fight, but yeah, this is a serious problem. Aside from anything else, that Ak'esh was the best chance we had to gaining further answers regarding the rituals, now it's as though we're back at square one.'

'Do you think there's anything in the idea of a mole? Someone freeing it on purpose?'

'On purpose? I can't think why. On the other hand, there's no way of accidentally freeing it either.' She sighed. 'I don't know what to think.'

They walked further into the facility together, the once optimistic atmosphere now cast away, replaced with only uncertainty, death, and dread for the days to come.

9

Four days later, with the base still on high alert and preparing to move to a new site at the end of the week, James was exercising in the facility's gym when a tap on the shoulder interrupted him. It was Ford. 'You're going to want to see this.' He swiftly led James in the direction of the control room. 'Sorry to interrupt your downtime, but this is important.'

'Have we had luck getting the security footage fixed?', James asked.

'Afraid not, but this blows that out of the water.'

James increased his pace, and presently they came to the entrance to the control room. It was abuzz with activity, men and women passing papers to one another, directing others to see to various tasks, still more seated at numerous computer screens, and all occasionally glancing at the images on the big screens before them.

'What is that?'

James could see an overhead image, clearly from a drone, showing multiple portals, except these were larger than those portals in photographs and footage he had been shown in the past, and unlike the usual purple, these were a pure mass of shimmering black, perhaps fifteen feet high, eighteen yards across wide. Three of them stood side by side in what appeared to be wilderness.

'Those are portals to the Otherworld,' replied Ford, 'But we've never had multiple ones open at once like that, nor have they ever been recorded as being that large or that colour. Oh, and you want to know the clincher? They've been open for the past hour.'

'What? Are you sure?'

'I wouldn't have said it if I wasn't. As far as we can see, these puppies have no intention of closing anytime soon. This is unprecedented, James, and we sure as shit don't know what it means.'

'Do we know their location?'

'We do,' answered Van Houten, having entered the control room. 'They have appeared in a stretch of woodland about two-hundred-and-fifteen miles west of Quebec. I am sending Alpha, Charlie, Bravo, and Echo to secure the site and pacify anything that tries coming through. See to your kit and meet with Crawford on the helipad, you leave in fifteen minutes. Oh, and I'm sending Agent Järvinen in with you to discern the nature of these new variants.'

James frowned upon hearing this. He knew that Anna was a veteran like himself, but she had never seen combat, let alone against the nightmares that were liable to confront them once there. 'Is that sensible, sir?'

'Of course it is,' Van Houten barked, 'She is one of our top intelligent analysts; I can think of no one better for the task.'

He swallowed. 'Yes, sir.'

Fifteen minutes later, James was in the air, a concerned look upon Crawford's face, Murphy deep in thought, and Anna smiling nervously at him. James did not return her look, feeling too anxious for her safety to do so. He cared for her, he knew it, he thought that she knew it too, and he felt an anger building up inside him towards Van Houten for putting her in the line of fire like this.

The noise of the helicopter was muffled due to the closed doors, but James wouldn't have heard it even if they hadn't been, such was his mind as it raced through the possible outcomes of this new development. As far as he knew, the NDA had never dealt with portals that failed to disappear after ten minutes, but if it was possible that these three wouldn't close at all, then the agency's entire approach to fighting the beings of the Otherworld might need to change. A sinking feeling gripped him as he contemplated another possibility. What if more of these potentially permanent portals appeared? How would they be able to hold off who knew how many vampires, werewolves, and God knows what else might seek to come through.

Time passed, they landed to refuel once in Canada, then the helicopters once more soared above the landscape in their rush to reach the portal site, a myriad of lakes and conifers littering the semi-wild landscape, becoming larger and thicker as the minutes wore on. After what seemed an age, the pilot informed them that they were five minutes away from the landing zone. With weapons checked, breath steadied, the doors were opened and Alpha team made contact with the hard soil once more. Around them, three other choppers made uneventful landings on the patch of grass that had been revealed amidst a sea of hardwood forest.

Once the din of the helicopters had lessened with their departure, the thirty operators made their way in line formation, entering an expanse of maple and birch, the forest floor littered in once green leaves, now rotting and coated with mud. Crawford informed them that they were two miles from the portal site, this having been the best landing site they could get.

'Stay close behind me,' James instructed Anna.

She gave him a thumbs up, then, with ever damper boots, the unit kept up the best pace possible, aware of the need to maintain visibility with one another, it being all too easy to become lost in the morass of timber. Overhead, the sky had become hidden in a blanket of grey clouds. Soon, they heard the sound of an almost indescribable whisper through the weathered boughs above them, as though something was powering up softly, gradually becoming louder with each yard more they trod.

As Crawford signalled to indicate that they were almost at their destination, the whisper seemed to reach a climax, morphing into a hiss that began to wear upon their ear drums.

'Is this normal?' asked James, close to Murphy's ear.

'The whispering was,' he replied, 'It stems from the portal, don't ask me why, but this hissing? I don't think that's normal, no.'

Ahead of them, they caught sight of three black shimmers amidst the never ending rows of ancient woodland through which they had hiked. Crawford rose his arm to call a halt, then signalled for the men to approach slowly, crouching low. Soon, their eyes made out the full extent of the scene before them, three enormous portals of shining ebony standing ominously ahead of them, perhaps no more than forty yards away. It appeared that the width of the portals had sundered or absorbed whatever flora had been present upon its opening, and as yet, no movement, only the unceasing hiss and shimmer of something altogether not of this world.

Movement ahead of them. Dazed groups of six or seven ragged looking Ak'esh stepped through from the portals, heads flitting about like birds.

'Shit,' muttered Crawford through his headset, 'All right, pick your targets, put them down on three.' Silence for several moments as sights were levelled on individual hostiles. 'One...two...three!'

A reverberation of gunfire tore through the Ak'esh, ripping their already torn clothing from their bodies, the mud of the forest floor intermixing with their splattered blood.

'Clear!' shouted Crawford, 'Command, proceeding forward to secure the portal site.'

The men rose, weapons raised, and as one unit began their approach towards the portal, those on the flanks scanned left and right to ensure that no Ak'esh had been missed. All appeared to be clear. The Ak'esh lay scattered about them, receiving further entry wounds to the head for their trouble, with Crawford admonishing someone for becoming distracted by the sight of the portal looming darkly above them.

'Command,' reported Crawford, 'Portals are secure, establishing a perimeter around the site.'

Whilst he gave orders to this effect, Anna, who had been keeping a safe distance behind the line of fire, now approached more confidently, notepad in hand, hurriedly scrawling notes on the portals, writing down any features not apparent on the drone footage. She took her camera, clasped around her neck via a lanyard, and began to take pictures, her face in awe, seemingly enjoying herself.

'Don't get too close, Anna,' warned James.

She ignored him, too much taken up in her work to hear. The hissing, all encompassing though it had been for the last ten minutes, seemed to defy belief and grow even louder now. James thought that it even sounded deliberate, rather than as a natural by-product of the portals function, as though something was trying to target their senses.

James turned to hear footsteps behind him. It was Nielsen, a recent recruit from Anna's home state. 'Sir, should we no—' Whatever he had been going to say was cut short as a blur of ashen blue swept between the two men in an instant. James could barely react, barely comprehend what had happened, wiping blood from his eyes before Nielsen fell backwards before him, desperately clasping his bloodied neck. James now leapt into action, dropping down low to try to staunch Nielsen's wound, the rivulets of his hands filling with rivers of red. 'Medic!' he yelled, but it was no use, weapons were being fired all around him, calls of 'Where the fuck is it?' and 'Stay low!' drowning out any cry for aid that he sought to make.

He looked back at Nielsen. 'Dan?' he asked, but it was no good; the kid was dead. He shouldered his rifle, looking around frantically for Anna, the fire having died down, but all he could see were the rest of the other field operatives, hunched down low to the ground, scanning the trees for movement. He caught sight of Ford, back to the ground, pistol pointing towards the sky. 'Ford, where's Anna?' he called.

'She...it took her, James.'

'What?'

'That thing...I think it was a Shrouded One...it grabbed her and took her through the portal.'

James felt weak upon hearing this, as though his legs were about to give way from under him. This couldn't be happening, not again, not Anna. His flurry of emotions, sickening in their intensity, coalesced into sudden anger. He raised his weapon and, with deliberate steps, began to move towards the portal.

'James, no!' called Ford.

'We have to go in after her, Calvin!'

A hand from his left grabbed the muzzle of his rifle, lowering it sharply, Crawford shoving his head angrily towards his own. 'You're under my command, Carlson, have you forgotten that? No one is going through that thing without authorisation, and I sure as shit am not requesting it.'

'Why the hell not?'

'Have you lost your senses? No one has ever been through to the Otherworld. Shit, we've never even had a portal open long enough to send a drone through. We have no idea what is waiting for us in there, do you not understand that? You could have an entire army of who knows what waiting for you on the other side. I get it, kid, I do, but you need to look at the situation as it is, not how you want it to be. I'm not saying that there's no hope here, but we do things by the book, understood? James, is that understood?'

He stared, his eyes wide, feeling a sense of frustration that he had never imagined possible. He gritted his teeth. 'Yes, sir, understood.'

***

Nielsen's body was flown back to headquarters, along with Alpha and Bravo teams, James sullen, feeling lower than he had felt in months.

'This ain't over, you know?' said Murphy, looking at James with concern.

'It damn well better not be,' came his reply. 'I don't care what they say, I'm going in after her.'

He nodded, exchanging a glance at Crawford who remained silent, staring out the window at the forest below. He had reported Anna's abduction to Command, but he had thought fit to keep their reply to himself.

Once back at Sandalwood, the two squads, still unbuckling their helmets, were met by Van Houten at the helipads, the sound of the rotor-blades gradually slowing to a halt in the background. 'I'm sorry that this happened, Jam—', he began, his words cut off by James's fury.

'We have to go and get her back, sir.'

'Just calm down, son.'

'This isn't a time to be calm, sir, it's a time to act! Every second we delay might make the difference between saving her or not. For Christ's sake, she might already be...' He broke off, unable to give voice to the words in his head.

Van Houten's expression grew hard. 'All right,' now addressing the men as a whole, 'Debriefing is in fifteen minutes.' With that, he turned on his heel and stalked back to the building, shaking his head irritably.

Upon joining the two squads in the debriefing room – a rectangular space furnished with half a dozen tables and a projector screen – James looked on expectantly as Van Houten addressed them. 'Listen,' he began, 'I understand what a loss Agent Järvinen is to us, I do, and if there is any chance that she might be brought back to our dimension by the forces that took her, then I will ensure that everything is done to rescue her from captivity.'

'I can't believe I'm hearing this...' muttered James.

Van Houten eyed him for a moment. 'As you all know, what we term the Otherworld has never been penetrated by United States forces or any other human agency. It is a known unknown; there is not a scrap of intelligence as to what forces a rescue attempt might face on the other side. After all these decades, all we know is that an all manner of nightmarish beings call it home. I encourage you all to consider the implications of what a rescue attempt would mean. It might very well be akin to invading Earth itself with a handful of men. That is the difficulty that I am faced with.'

He paused to take a breath, staring at the table for a moment. 'I'm sorry, truly I am, but there will be no rescue mission through the portals. Our priority is to monitor the status of the three portals and guard against further incursions into our world.'

'This is a fucking disgrace,' muttered James ruefully.

'You can call it what you like Agent Carlson, but it *is* my order, therefore it *is final*, is that understood?' he said, his voice rising in anger.

'Yes, sir, perfectly.'

'Good. Dismissed.'

The men of Alpha and Brave filed out of the room, James shaking his head in disbelief at what he saw as an utter betrayal. He had been taught in the Army that no one was ever to be left behind, yet now they were proposing leaving Anna to the wolves. He felt sick just thinking about it. But what, he asked himself, could he do?

As dusk fell that evening, he lay awake, the very thought of falling asleep being unthinkable at such a time. His entire world had once again fallen apart, the colour having been replaced with a turgid grey that seemed to pick away at his very being. He knew that he had to pull himself together. Anna was still out there, somehow he had to get her back. He held up a photograph that she had given him, the image showing the two of them smiling together during a hike they had taken in the forest surrounding Sandalwood. He quickly placed the picture back down, unable to bear looking at it for a second longer.

His misery was interrupted by a knock on the door. He put the photo in his pocket absentmindedly before responding.

'Yeah?'

It opened, revealing Murphy, Ford, and the rest of Alpha and Bravo, excluding Crawford who was noticeably absent.

'What is it?'

'Got a moment?', asked Murphy.

James stood up and walked over to the door. 'Do you have news?'

He shook his head. 'Van Houten's still adamant about his decision.'

'Fucking prick...'

'But screw his decision,' said Murphy with an intense look in his eyes.

James's heart began to beat faster as his hope was renewed. 'Yeah?'

'Yeah. The way we see it, this isn't just about getting Anna back. See, that thing that took her, that killed Nielsen, we reckon it's got to be the same Shrouded One that kept appearing in the vicinity of those rituals.'

James nodded, taking in every word.

'So, three portals appear at the same time these rituals have been happening, portals that don't disappear like they're supposed to; it means something.' There was a murmur of agreement behind him. 'Then I asked myself, why did that thing take Anna through the portal? It could have killed her outright like it did to Nielsen, but it didn't, why?'

'You're saying it could be connected to the rituals?'

'Sorry to say it, James, but yes.'

'Fucking hell...'

'That's why we're proposing to say F-you to Van Houten and go in anyway.'

James's head snapped up. 'Really? I mean, thank you, all of you, but how?'

'Michaels and Krieghoff are going to take us out there within the hour, as soon as it's dark. We have access to the armoury, and they're willing to be fired, or worse, if it means sticking two fingers up to Van Houten's decision.'

'I'm going to stay behind to work on Van Houten,' said Ford. 'It's going to be like a nuke going off when he learns of this, and we're going to need someone here batting for our side. I doubt he'll see reason, but I can try.'

James ran his eyes across the awaiting faces of his brothers-in-arms, nodding slowly. 'Let's do it.'

Within the hour, M4s, shotguns, and as much ammunition as they could carry had been quietly ferried outside and loaded onto the two helicopters. A few eyebrows had been raised, but most of the remaining staff were used to operations taking place night and day, thinking better than to stick their noses into things.

As the last members of the squads were making their way up the steps to the helipad, James watched on, suddenly overcome with a feeling of intense respect for those around him, more so than usual, for it struck him that they were willing to march into what very well might be hell in order to rescue someone dear to him.

'All right,' shouted Murphy, patting the pilot on the shoulder, 'Let's get underway.'

Just as he was closing the side-door of the chopper, James caught sight of Crawford, his face snarling in anger as he realised what was happening.

'Go, go, go', yelled James, Crawford already having broken out into a sprint to try to reach them. He was too late; within seconds they were airborne, turning in the direction of Canada, a dark vista before them, praying that they would not be too late.

10

The two helicopters circled noisily above the portals, terrified birds fleeing from the canopy below, moonlight bathing the spinning helix in a ghostly light. Every second mattered, so they had dispensed with their earlier landing zone, electing to conduct a fast-rope descent directly over the target. All appeared clear as they circled the area, muzzles trained below in case more hostiles were lying in wait. On Murphy's command, they began their descent to the forest floor, the first man down readying his weapon to the left, James following swiftly behind and panning to his right. Once they were all on the ground, the helicopters took off to find a suitable landing zone, having agreed to remain within the boundaries of radio contact if and when the squads returned.

James stared at the largest of the three portals, huddled between the smaller two. There was something truly malevolent, he felt, about its dark, unnatural appearance. It was something altogether beyond his understanding... and he was about to go through it.

'All right,' said Murphy, his voice urgent, 'There might be no coming back from this, so if anyone has second thoughts about going through this thing, then speak up now, you won't be thought any less for it.' Not a soul stepped forward. 'I didn't think so,' he smiled. 'Once we're through, execute a one-hundred-and-eighty degree sweep of the area. After that, well, we'll cross that bridge when we come to it.'

He turned, joined by James and soon the others, sixteen men in total. 'I hope we're doing the right thing,' he whispered.

'We are,' said James confidently.

'All right, age before beauty.' He stepped into the portal, disappearing in an instant. James stared for half a second, then put his right leg forward, vanishing in turn.

James opened his eyes, his face suddenly far colder than it had been moments before, specks of something small and dainty landing against his cheeks. He was taken aback by what he saw. All around him, accompanied each second by more and more of his comrades, was an expanse of rugged terrain, in some ways familiar, in others utterly alien. In the distance, he saw, enormous creatures, their dark red wings spanning what he guessed must be sixteen feet across, were soaring in the distance amid dark mountain peaks and leaden clouds. He realised that it was ash landing on his cheek; the atmosphere was choked with it.

The portal was located on a promontory, around which spread an inland sea as far as the eye could gauge; a dark mirror reflecting a darker firmament.

The entire land seemed like something dreamt up by an evil mind, and James shuddered to think that Anna had been taken somewhere farther into this place.

'Welcome to the Otherworld' said Murphy, walking up to him, 'No wonder they're all so eager to leave.'

'It looks like there's a high point about a few miles up that gorge,' James said, pointing to a valley of half-dead trees and twisted parody's of pine forest. 'Looks like as good a place as any to check out.'

'All right, take point.' Then addressing the others, 'Let's move out; we've got a friend to save.'

The terrain was arid, coarse, and devoid of flora beyond wisps of what might have been called grass, though to call it 'alive' would have been a stretch. It was as if this hellscape was as devoid of heart as the inhabitants of it, any life-force that lingered having been subject to the depredations of jealous souls wont to stamp out its beauty. A sense of dread lingered with every step the strangers took, as though each new yard was an affront to some unseen, ancient evil. After a mile, the terrain grew steeper, and upwards they trekked amid rock and dead blades of a species doubtless unknown to man. In the distance, the harsh screams of the avian devils gave the travellers recourse to turn every few yards, their guard never dropping for a moment.

As they came to the crest of a hill, they hit the ground upon seeing what lay below. James wasn't sure what he had been expecting, but he was shocked to see the extent of whatever civilisation appeared to call this place home.

A small town, like something out of a textbook on the medieval era, lay below. The architecture, such as it was, appeared to be comprised of rotting timber, the houses being more akin to shacks. Throughout the dirt-strewn streets were torches flickering in the waning light. He took out his binoculars, beginning to scan the streets, following it, higher and higher, until his vision became obscured by a mass of rock, wood, and stone that comprised what could only be described as a fortress or stronghold. Among the paths leading to and fro, James gazed upon the inhabitants. He turned to Murphy, 'I don't know what I'm looking at, but you need to see this.' He passed the binoculars, watching as Murphy began to frown upon seeing the same multitude of humanoids that apparently called this place home.

They were about six feet in height, he estimated, with no hair to speak of, a sickly green skin, teeth like sharpened rocks, and blood red eyes. No one at Sandalwood had mentioned anything like them, but James thought it best to assume hostility.

'Well I'll be damned,' remarked Murphy.

'What?' asked James.

'Take a look.' He handed him the binoculars. 'End of the main street, by the front door on the left.'

James watched as four beings, clearly Ak'esh, strode over to a group of the humanoids, one of them proceeding to batter a bystander, seemingly at random, until it lay still, not a sign of life to be seen.

'You thinking what I'm thinking?' he asked.

'I hope not,' replied Murphy, 'We don't have a clue what these things are; they could want nothing more than to eat us for all we know.'

'You make a good point, but take a look about you.' He gestured left and right, the landscape showing only mile upon mile of swampland, mountains, and lakes, nothing else suggesting civilisation of any kind as far as the eye could see. 'If Anna was taken anywhere, then this is our best bet, and if the Ak'esh treat these 'people' anywhere as badly as they treat us, then maybe we can reason with them.'

'James, they won't even be able to speak English, how exactly do you plan to reason with them?'

'Hey, I never said it was without flaws, but what options do we have here? Seriously?'

Murphy looked around, aware that others in the team were looking on in expectation of orders. 'Shit. All right, how are we going to do this?'

James looked ahead. 'It looks like we can stick close to the line of boulders on the left. There's not much cover, I know, but it's the best we have. That'll get us within fifty or sixty yards of the settlement, and from then on we'll just have to hope for the best. It's not like I see any surveillance cameras around to pick us up.'

With every man resolved to the plan, they made their way, one after the other, crouching low as they crossed across the rocky ground to the large span of dark grey boulders, some split as though by some angry god, staying close to the wall as they followed its line of advance. Upon reaching the end of the rock formation, they formed a line, so as to limit their visibility upon approach, and began to run the last stretch to the town, breaking into a sprint the closer they came to it.

Once there, they hit the dirt, their eyes moving from left to right to see if they had been spotted. Amazingly, it appeared as though they had not been. Using hand signals, Murphy gestured for eight men to follow him, James being one of them, while the rest remained behind to provide cover. Another short sprint, and James found himself with his back against a dilapidated shack, the main street beginning just to his left.

'All right, what's our next move?' he asked.

'You're asking me? I thought you knew,' Murphy replied.

'I did, up until this point anyway.'

'Quiet!' He froze as footsteps began to foretell of something coming their way.

Without second guessing himself, James moved to the edge of the shack, listening as each step became nearer and nearer, then, just as he saw the form of a creature begin to appear in front of him, he reached forward quickly, grabbed its tattered clothing, and wrenched it backwards behind the shack.

He instinctively had his hand over the creature's mouth, all thought as to infection or the loss of his fingers having left his mind. He held up a finger to silence it. It's red, otherworldly eyes, pupils like those of a panicked snake, stared intently at this pale appendage before it, then turned to look into his own. It struck him that it seemed to understand what was being asked of it, and slowly, hesitantly, he began to lower his hand.

The creature did not cry out, nor did it try to run, it simply continued to watch with curiosity.

'I don't suppose you speak English?' James said.

It tilted its head questioningly.

'Didn't think so.' He reached into his pocket, suddenly remembering that he had left Anna's picture there from when Murphy had visited his quarters. He held it for the creature to see, it's eyes widening slightly upon seeing her image. He tapped the photo. 'We're here for her. Her name's Anna. Have you seen this woman?'

The creature appeared to become more animated, its jaw opening and closing, as if trying to communicate.

'You have seen her?' James asked eagerly.

Again, the creature's jaw gesticulated, a vague rasp being what little speech it seemed capable of. It held out its clawed hands, three fingers on each, and beckoned for him to follow.

'Woah, hold on,' began Murphy, but James cut him short.

'Like you said, what options do we have?'

The creature's eyes darted from one to the other, ignorant of their words.

'James, we don't have a clue what this thing might do, it could want to walk us out into the open and then call the Ak'esh to finish us off.'

'After they just beat his buddy to death? Really?'

The creature held up a scaly hand, pointing at the photograph of Anna, then gesturing behind him in the direction of the fortress.

'Anna's there?' James asked.

The creature did not appear to answer, instead gesturing for them to wait.

'I think we should do what it says.'

'Ah God...this is nuts,' said Murphy.

James heard some of the other men groan in what he took to be disapproval, so he looked around to address them. 'Look where we are, look around you. The very fact that we're here is nothing short of a miracle, so why not bet just slightly more on our luck holding out for us? I don't know whether to trust this thing or not, but it seems to know where Anna is, and right now I don't see what other option we have.'

'All right,' said Murphy grudgingly, 'Let it go.'

The creature felt James relinquishing his grip altogether, and with a few more mouth movements in what he hoped was a gesture of thanks, it walked around the corner onto the main street.

'I hope you know what you're doing,' muttered Murphy.

'So do I.'

Shortly afterwards, accompanied by seven other beings of its kind, the creature returned with what appeared to be a large, makeshift cart, full of what James reluctantly came to think were some sort of enormous skins, stacked in layers, as though serving the function of tarpaulin. The creature pointed to the men, then to the cart.

'You've got to be kidding me,' said Murphy. 'They want to Trojan Horse this thing?'

'What choice do we have? Anyone? James asked.

No one spoke.

'We're going up there anyway, at least this way we might have the benefit of surprise. If we get a whiff of betrayal then we'll fling over the covering and they can be the first to eat a bullet.'

'I don't like this, James.'

'Neither do I, but it's the best option open to us.'

With stern looks and much biting of lips, the interlopers from Earth climbed into the cart from behind the cover of the shack, their world becoming darkness once it was draped over them. From then on, it was a question of patience and holding their nerve. They felt the wheels of the cart trundle along the path, smelled the pungent odour in the cart, and heard strange voices in an unknown tongue calling out to their unexpected allies.

They tried their best to remain still, holding on to anything they could in order to steady themselves, the cart having begun to tilt as it made its laboured journey up the slope to the fortress's entrance.

After what might have been near on ten minutes, but felt more like an hour, the cart came to a sudden halt. Rasping voices called out in their direction. James recognised the word 'Ak'esh', and listened as their cart-bearers replied to whatever had been demanded of them. With immense relief, the cart began to trundle on, coming to another stop after about another two minutes of nervous waiting.

Without warning, the skin covering was pulled back, revealing the expectant face of their initial helper, whom Murphy had taken to calling 'Snake Eyes'. James took the animated opening and shutting of Snake Eyes's mouth as an indication that the coast was clear. Slowly, he peered out from the cart, freezing for a moment upon finding himself confronted with louring walls of dark stone and rotting timber, soaring upwards of three hundred feet or more above him. He turned, finding that the same walls enclosed them entirely. He realised that they had been brought into the fortress's courtyard.

'Where are the guards?' he said out loud.

'Maybe they never thought they needed any? These guys seem peaceful enough, and it doesn't look like there's anyone else around here for them to worry about,' said Murphy.

'All right, here goes nothing.' He climbed out of the cart, carrying his rifle in one hand, then he levelled it at the scores of windows watching their every move. No movement, barely a sound other than the noise of boots hitting the ground and the tortured breaths of Snake Eyes's kin.

'Where to now?' asked James, directing his question towards their helper.

Snake Eyes looked blank, unsure what it was that he was being asked.

'You don't know, huh? All right, we'll find a way in. Murph, I'll take point.'

'Copy.'

A man-sized slab of carved rock seemed more like an entrance than anything else that caught James's eye. He made his way there, his buddies' rifles covering him from every possible angle as they joined him.

'Now where are they going?' asked Murphy in alarm.

James turned, noticing that Snake Eyes and the other creatures were leaving with the cart. 'I guess they can't afford to risk staying any longer.'

'How nice for them...'

'Come on, let's make entry.'

Without another word, James found a groove in the right side of the slab. He clasped the cold stone with his fingers, pulled towards him, and found that it slowly began to give way, dust beginning to fall softly from above. Accompanied by another pointman, the two entered the fortress, James turning left, the other man right, both covering what they found was a long hallway of stone slabs, some sort of red mineral comprising the walls, and flames that, to their amazement, appeared to float in mid air with no discernible means of support.

Once everyone was inside, it was decided that two men, Rogers and Massaro, would stay behind to cover their exit, while the other sixteen would press onwards and see what they could find. They pressed onwards through the dark walls of the structure, a stench of death invading their nostrils, their steps echoing through the cavernous tunnels, their shadows keeping pace as they searched for some semblance of a passageway. They were panting when they finally came across it, an open stairwell consisting of three feet wide stone slabs, spiraling upwards left to right. One man recoiled upon seeing the macabre display of red eyes hanging neatly from the walls, fixed there by crosses, the product of some sick mind beyond their comprehension. At least they now knew, thought James, that there was little doubt that their new friends could be trusted.

James led the way, rifle raised, taking each hard step as it came, anticipating contact with each new angle of the staircase. He was aware of every impact of his boots, much as he might try to muffle his footsteps. He forced himself not to notice the tortured eyes around him, seemingly pleading for help where there could of course be none. A flame-lit opening appeared ahead of him, mirror image of that which had been found below, and he stepped forward into the chamber beyond.

The chamber was large, austere, and cold. A fire burned large from a hearth of jagged rock, spitting flames and warming their faces.

'Something's not right. This was too easy,' remarked James.

'I'll consider it easy once we're back in Canada,' said Murphy.

They stepped forward into the room, noticing another doorway on the opposite end. Upon crossing the halfway point, however, the calm was ruptured by a sudden wall of stone slicing its way through the middle of the chamber from some unseen gap behind the hearth. Only five men had made it across with them, the other eleven finding themselves cut off on the other side, a blaring of gunfire resounding from behind the stone barrier.

'Shit!' Murphy cried, the seven of them trying to find some way of opening the wall, frantically feeling the stone itself, as well as examining their side of the hearth for some sort of mechanism, but it was no use, there was nothing that they could do.

'They're being killed over there!' Murphy yelled, the shouts and screams of his friends being all too audible amidst the sound of shotgun blasts and rifle fire.

'We can't get through this way, let's try to find another way around!' shouted James, leading the way as they charged towards the exit, his heart dropping as they found yet another stairwell leading to a third floor.

'Fuck! Where do we go from here?' asked one of their number.

'We go forward, maybe there's a route back around to them,' replied James.

Their path forward seemed to only lead upwards, no path back down to the lower levels being apparent. At the point at which they were reaching a state of abject dejection, however, James stopped at what he thought was a sob. He held up a hand, the others stopped, and then a fair-haired operative remarked that he heard it too.

'It's coming from down this hall,' said James, hastening to the end of it. He came to another stone slab, found purchase with his fingers, and tightened his muscles as he pulled it back towards him. Ahead of him, he could have shouted out of both horror and relief, since there, on the other end of the dimly furnished chamber, was Anna. She was slumped against the floor, breathing faintly, her wrists bound and fettered to the wall. Around her were dark grey fonts carved of stone, some sort of dark, thick liquid bubbling in their basins, and the ominous words '*Math'ok Kalah Ak'esh*' dripping from the wall. He threw caution to the wind, dashing forward to reach her, kneeling down whilst the others covered his six.

'Anna! Anna, we're here,' he said, clasping her shoulders and checking her for injuries, particularly her neck. 'What did they do to you? Oh God, I'm so glad you're alive.'

117

She coughed, opening one of her eyelids slowly. Her eyes were bloodshot, yet it did not appear that she had been bitten by an Ak'esh or otherwise. Instead, it appeared that she had been badly beaten, the skin around her face dark and bruised, with small cuts here and there. He felt the softness of her skin as he inspected the wounds, taking out a medical pack from his pocket and seeing to the cuts.

She winced as she felt her wounds being disinfected, the brown antiseptic liquid dripping down her cheek. 'You came,' she whispered.

'We were never going to leave you, Anna.'

She coughed weakly. 'She'll come for us, James.'

'Who? Just take it easy, Anna, we'll get you out of here.'

'Tash'ka, the Shrouded One, she's behind all this.'

'Behind what?'

'The plan, the rituals, it's all her, James.' Again she was interrupted by a fit of coughing, but it seemed to coincide with a surge in her resolve. She clasped his collar and met his eyes. 'We have to kill her, James.'

'Trust me, if I see her, she's dead.'

'No... we need to kill her before we leave this place, or else she'll succeed in opening more portals. It's her plan, James, she told me so.'

'Told you what exactly?'

'That she figured out the ritual to create portals to Earth. She needed me... a human sacrifice... she didn't know until now, but it needed to be done here, not on Earth.'

'How is that possible?'

She smiled grimly through her half-closed eye. 'We're not in Kansas anymore, James; the old rules don't apply.'

'All right, let's get you up first.' He turned to Murphy. 'How can we get these chains off her?'

'Tash'ka, she has the key,' answered Anna.

'Where is she? How can we find her?' asked James.

She pointed upwards with scarred hands. 'Up, keep going up.' Her head slunk downwards again.

'Anna? Anna? She's blacked out.'

'Okay,' said Murphy, 'We need someone to stay with her.'

'I'll stay, sir,' said Stokes, a capable man from Bravo team, his heavily lined face determined and alert.

He nodded, holding his firearm upright and looking at the remaining four of his squad, 'Alright, let's finish this.'

They returned to the hallway. Upon finding the next staircase, sweat beading down their brows, they made their way ever higher into this lair of darkness. James was aware that the Ak'esh that ambushed the rest of the squad were likely searching for them, and he immediately regretted leaving only Stokes to defend her. That said, with what he knew about Shrouded Ones, they would need as much support as he could get.

'We must be nearing the top of this place soon,' remarked Schweitzer, a nervous look on the careworn New Jerseyite's face.

'Wait,' said James.

'What?' asked Murphy.

'You don't hear that?'

The six men listened, tilting their heads to focus for anything other than the ever-present crackling of embers.

'Whispering, I hear it,' said Murphy.

'Same as when we first arrived at the portal, and you know who swooped in after that,' said James.

'This is what they want, for us to lose our heads; let's keep it together, boys.'

The next spiral staircase appeared different to the rest. No longer the cramped space flanked on either side by the fortress's walls, this staircase had been built in an ornate wood-pannelled room, a dark-wood banister extending the dimensions of the second floor. It gave James the impression of a library in some Ivy League university, or rather some twisted simulacrum of one. Darkness had largely claimed the expansive room for its own, yet on both sides of the stairs, as well as in front of it, stood iron braziers emitting a fierce heat, the men shielding their faces with gloved hands to ward it off.

'Doesn't look like this leads anywhere other than up, ' said Murphy. 'Let's move to the second floor; Schweitzer, Henriksen, cover our rear.'

The steps began to creak with each cautious step that James took, gritting his teeth in frustration with every unintended alarm they brought forth. A smell of what he could only compare with incense wafted through the air. As soon as he saw that his immediate left and right were clear, he and Murphy turned to face the open space of the second floor, opposite the stairs. James immediately raised his rifle at what lay ahead of him, for twenty-five yards away, flanked by marble columns and seated upon a jagged throne, sat the Shrouded One.

Her throne was a twelve feet high monstrosity of skulls and ligaments, bound together through some ancient art of darkness, six feet wide braziers burning fiercely either side of the demon herself, the whole illuminated from above by sickly rays of light. James caught her eyes, as black as death itself, her ashen grey skin amidst robes of black, dark hair falling in unkempt locks, an unholy creation from which stared an icy hatred.

The six men kept her firmly in their sights, dark boots putting one foot cautiously in front of the other as they continued their advance.

Her lips began to part in a wry smile, her black fangs illuminated by the shadows of the flames. 'You have come to claim Tash'ka's head as your trophy, I see.'

None of them said a word, instead coming to a halt and readying themselves to fire.

'Why fight me?', her strangely sonorous voice asked of them. 'You would not be the first to serve me, nor would you be the last.'

James frowned. 'Not the first? What are you talking about?'

Her head turned sharply, fixing him in her gaze. 'Our purpose in your world requires aid from your kind. The Ak'esh, through my guidance, can offer you much, can offer you immortality. Another saw this truth, saw to our aid, and so too can you all.'

'What is this demon blabbering about?' snarled Murphy, preparing to pull his trigger.'

'Wait!' shouted James. He took a step forward, 'Who is helping you on Earth? Give us a name.'

Her smile died away, leaving only contempt behind it. 'You will not join us? Then your bodies shall serve as a feast to your goddess.'

In a second of hearing her words, bullets were shattering the throne upon which she had sat, shards of bone and viscera scattering heavily in all directions, but none hitting their intended target. She was fast, amazingly so, and now their muzzles turned wildly this way and that, upwards at all angles, trying to keep track with the blur of grey as it soared throughout the room. James watched as Schweitzer's head was severed in front of him, his body dropping heavily to the floor, like a doll with its strings cut, a pool of blood spreading rapidly around it.

The room was a deafening cacophony of sound: bullets impacting the columns and ceiling structure, splinters of wood falling onto their heads, screams as more men were cruelly sliced by the sharp wings and claws that seemed to travel from one side of the room to another in the blink of an eye.

'We can't hit her!' cried Henriksen.

'We've got to, keep firing!' shouted James.

Only a moment passed before Henriksen fell face forward on the floor, savage claws having cleaved a bloody chunk from the back of his now shattered skull.

They were down to their last magazines, and in desperation, roaring like lions, the remaining four NDA operatives unleashed hell upon their foe, leading the target as best they could, giving everything they had to bring her down. Without warning, a scream of pain and rage filled their eardrums, the men wincing in pain as they struggled to continue their rate of fire. They had hit her, James realised, seeing the blur slow down, small drops of dark blood landing on the wooden floorboards. Suddenly, the blur slammed into the left-hand corner of the throne-room, revealing the writhing figure of Tash'ka, her bat-like wings torn to shreds, her body riddled with holes.

They closed in, not taking any more chances, showering her with led until chunks of her face lay about her body, not a flicker to be seen from her limbs.

Murphy spat, breathing heavily. 'Now, let's get the hell out of this God forsaken place.'

In spite of their exhaustion, the four men ran in their efforts to retrace their steps, coming swiftly to the room wherein Anna had been kept prisoner. James felt a swell of relief upon seeing her once more, alive and conscious, Stokes supporting her on his shoulder.

'Is she dead?' asked Anna with hopeful eyes.

'She's dead,' replied James.

'Where are the others?'

He shook his head.

She dropped her head sadly. 'I'm so sorry this had to happen.'

'It's nothing you did, Anna, don't even say that. It was all that demon's doing. We have to go now; are you okay to move?'

'Her leg's badly bruised,' said Stokes.

'I'll be all right, I can make it,' she replied.

'All right,' declared Murphy, 'Let's get a move on.'

The small group began their descent through the stronghold, retracing their steps as best they could, spurred on by the elation of success, and the awareness that stealth had long since gone out the window. Soon, they came to a hallway with two entrances, left and right. The dead body of an Ak'esh was lying halfway between the arch on the right, and through it they found the room where they had become separated from the others.

It had been a massacre. All eleven men now lay dead, torn and bitten savagely by the Ak'esh, yet they had given them hell for their trouble, for among them were littered the snarling faces of dead vampires, some stabbed to death, some shot, others pummeled with rifle butts. There was nothing they could do for them, so reluctantly they continued down the stairwell behind them.

Upon reaching the ground floor, they once more found the door through which they had entered, rejoining Massaro and Rogers.

'Where are the others?' asked Massaro 'It sounded like the Fourth of July up there.'

'We're all that's left,' replied Jack grimly.

Massaro closed his eyes, then patted Rogers on the shoulder to get moving. The courtyard still silent, nothing but a soft cry of the wind about them. It felt a relief for them all to finally be outside again, even if it was in this alien environment. They jogged to the archway leading out of the courtyard, turned a corner, and found that the path towards the village appeared clear.

'The Ak'esh guarding the entrance must have been part of the ambush,' suggested Murphy.

James nodded. 'Let's keep moving.'

As they moved as fast as they could through the settlement's main thoroughfare, taking turns to support Anna on their shoulders, they paid little attention to the inhabitants' questioning eyes. It seemed to James, however, that the creatures sensed their success, for, as one, they began to emit a mournful wail that stopped them short for a moment.

'What are they doing?' asked Murphy.

'Maybe they're thanking us?' suggested James.

'Screw it, as long as they stay out of our way, they can sing as much as they want.'

With that, they bid farewell to the settlement, retracing their steps for the mile it took to reach the earlier high point, Anna wincing in pain throughout, James gritting his teeth in desperation to get her medical attention. After what seemed a gargantuan effort, their feet tiredly taking each step up the arid hillside, a mistimed grip occasionally causing their feet to slide backwards and stumble, they reached the top. From there, it was easier going, the land levelling out until, after about half a mile, it began the final descent back towards the lake and their exit portal.

'Is that who I think it is?' asked Murphy, squinting.

James looked towards the portal, utterly taken aback upon seeing another human being, dressed similarly to themselves, apparently waiting for them. 'Is that... is that Crawford?'

'Looks like him.'

'The madman actually followed us through?' James remarked, smiling at the daring of his commander.

Murphy grinned, still bemused at what he was seeing, and together the eight survivors traversed distance between them and the portal, their spirits high in spite of all that they had suffered and lost to get there.

'Commander Crawford?' asked James as they neared the awaiting figure, an amazed smile on his face.

'Did you kill Tash'ka?' came Crawford's bland reply.

James's smile fell away, replaced with a questioning look. 'We did, sir... how did you know her name?'

Crawford stared, slowly nodding his head, his jaw clenched tightly. "You... stupid bastard!' he shouted after a moment, drawing his sub-machine gun like lightening, blowing away the brains of two of Alpha team in an instant, wounding Massaro and Rogers, and firing a bullet squarely into James's chest before anyone could react. Anna dived for cover, finding little of anything that would do, while Murphy and Stokes managed to get two shots off before they, too, were hit by Crawford's fire. Murphy took the impact on his shoulder, seeing his chance when Crawford began to reload, and charging forwards without a second's thought. He knocked Crawford to the ground, the two men beginning to grapple desperately, Crawford's fingers attempting to press down into Murphy's eyes, their mouths agape, rasping as one sought to subdue the other.

'You couldn't have just left it alone could you!' spat Crawford, seeming to gain the upper hand over his already exhausted subordinate. 'You took her from me, well now I'll take yo—'

His final word was blown to the wind, along with much of his skull and frontal lobe. The two men collapsed. Murphy turned to see James lying on the ground three yards away, his sidearm still raised.

Murphy was in shock, unable to speak.

'We'll deal with this later,' said James, 'Let's just get out of here first.'

Murphy helped James up, then the two of them supported Anna and Stokes, along with Rogers and Massaro doing the same to each other. There were no final looks back, no sentimental speeches, they simply stepped through the dark, shimmering mass eagerly, never wanting to see this nightmare again.

11

An instant passed, and once again they were back in the dark woods of Quebec, the air colder but, somehow, welcome; the hoot of a nearby owl as sweet to their ears as the finest of songs.

Anna sat on the damp ground, her hands becoming muddied; she began to nurse her injured leg. Murphy immediately pulled out his radio and began his attempt to make contact with Michaels and Krieghoff. Meanwhile, James eased himself down next to Anna. 'Are you all right?' he asked.

'I'll live,' she replied. 'I wish I could say the same about the others.'

James nodded, suddenly hit by the enormity of his fellow operatives' sacrifice. 'They knew the risks,' he finally said, 'We all did... and we were willing to take them.'

She nodded sadly, then raised her head to look at him. 'Crawford, he knew Tash'ka by name.'

'So he was the mole; he released the Ak'esh that night.'

She shook her head in disbelief. 'Why would he do that?'

'Back in the fortress, when we confronted Tash'ka, she spoke about offering us immortality, and how another one of us had taken her up on the offer. He must have been worried that the Ak'esh would reveal more of Tash'ka's plan. Earlier, I noticed Crawford holding a picture of a little girl; she looked like she had leukemia.'

'I didn't know he had a daughter.'

'Well, whoever she is, it looked as if she meant a whole lot to him. It also looked like there wasn't a lot of hope for her. Maybe we'll never know for sure, but my guess? Somehow, Tash'ka made contact with him, presented an offer of immortality for the girl, and in desperation he took it to save her. I don't think it was Tash'ka he was referring to when he said that we took her from him.'

'But to help in the enslavement of humanity for the sake of his child?' she asked, appalled.

He stared into her eyes meaningfully. 'Love can make us do terrible things, Anna... as well as great things.'

The moment was interrupted by Murphy announcing that the pilots were on their way. 'How are you holding up?' he asked Anna.

'I'm all right.'

'Stokes?'

'They can't kill me that easily,' he replied with a grimace.

Soon, the survivors of mankind's first foray into the Otherworld began to hear the familiar beat of helicopter rotor-blades, drawing nearer on the ever lightening horizon.

'Van Houten will be glad to hear we made it,' remarked Anna.

James looked briefly away. 'Yeah...about that.'

'What?'

'This rescue mission wasn't exactly authorised by the relevant authorities.'

'Oh?'

'Yeah, we might have stolen the choppers.'

'Well... I'm glad you did.'

He smiled. 'At least we can tell him that we stopped Earth from being invaded by untold numbers of Tash'ka's portals, that's got to count for something.'

She placed her hand on his, the sun beginning to edge its way above the dark disk ahead of them, its welcome rays bathing the new dawn and surrounding woodland in a warm glow. The shadow of two choppers briefly travelled over them, circling overhead, then an unexpected third brought the image of a grinning Ford raising his fist triumphantly from the side door.

'You know what, Anna?' James said with a smile.

'What's that?'

'I think the colour is starting to come back into my world again.'

Printed in Great Britain
by Amazon

33415773R00076